# Chimney Rock BLUES

## Janet McClellan

THE NAIAD PRESS, INC.
1999

Printed in the United States of America on acid-free paper
First Edition

Editor: Lila Empson
Cover designer: Bonnie Liss (Phoenix Graphics)
Typesetter: Sandi Stancil


**Library of Congress Cataloging-in-Publication Data**

McClellan, Janet, 1951 –
    Chimney Rock blues / by Janet McClellan.
        p.      cm. — (A Tru North mystery ; 4)
    ISBN 1-56280-233-X  (alk. paper)
    I. Title.  II. Series: McClellan, Janet, 1951 –    Tru North
mystery ; 4.
PS3563.C3413C47   1999
813'.54—dc21                                          98-44754
                                                          CIP

*To B.J.,*
*who helped me and others*
*bring murderers to justice.*

*Are you still out there good heart,*
*or did time run out?*

## About the Author

Janet McClellan is a twenty-five-year-plus veteran in the criminal justice field. Her experiences range from patrol officer, detective, college professor, and prison administrator, to chief of police. Not in Kansas anymore, Janet McClellan went north, at last, to the Oregon coast. Her previous works include *K.C. Bomber, Penn Valley Phoenix, River Quay,* and *Windrow Garden.*

# Chapter 1

An hour into the journey, Valerie Blake began to long for the simple comforts of the Jackson County Jail. The security harness across her shoulders and lap had begun to chafe her nerves more than her body. The cuffs of steel that held her hands securely in front of her were double-locked to a thick canvas belt wrapped around her waist. The thin padding of the bus seat, with its hard plastic upholstery, made the bouncing and swaying of the bus only slightly bearable.

She shifted and tugged at the bright orange jump-suit. It was ill fitting. The one-size-fits-all of prison clothes was a joke. She swam in the folds of her clothing. Valerie wondered what would have been so wrong with letting her wear her blue jeans and sweater. The cuffs and chains certainly seemed to assure her cooperation in the transport.

Valerie glanced out between the narrow, parallel slats of the security windows and tried to catch a glance at the passing greenery. She let out a deep sigh. The morning was a blur of confusion and her destination a complete mystery.

The women jailers had come to her cell before sunrise. They had directed her to stand, subjected her to the indignities of a strip search, and then rudely ordered her to get dressed. They hurried her along the narrow row of cells until someone shoved a paper sack with egg sandwiches into her hands and then left her to wait in a dimly-lit holding cell. None of her hustling guards offered to answer her questions, although they had made hushed threats when she ventured to raise her voice in protest. She fell silent and waited uncertainly for her fate to arrive. The creeping cold in the cinder-block confinement reminded her of how little sleep she'd had in three weeks.

The stern, unsmiling faces and the intent of the movements of her guards were all she had to tell her that something was in the works. Finally they came for her and walked her out to the waiting bus. She stumbled briefly from the short chains around her ankles as she tried to match their pace.

On the bus, other prisoners huddled in the gloom and raised their masculine voices in hoots and whistles. She was placed in the tiny, steel-lined cell at the front of the bus as the voices from the dim interior heartily complained about her remoteness from them. She shivered. She was not cold, although the air was humid. The persistent suggestions from the rumbling voices of her fellow passengers unnerved her. She hated their rudeness, their smells, and their assertions of dominance over her and others like her. She closed her ears to their caterwauling and felt herself drift from the time and place of her detention.

Disappearing through her mind — being some other place, some other time — was an old trick. She had used it often enough when growing up. It was survival, a means of escape when no one and nothing of peace or safety was left to her. Most of the time she could surrender herself to it at will. That was when the memories only threatened, when they crept toward her and she knew they were coming. But much of the time they were a dull roar hammering at the back of her mind. They would wait for a lapse of attention and come to her in dreams and visions. Then she would drown them as quickly as she could in alcohol. Her slowly growing dependency on drowning her fear and self-hate had begun to submerge her and her life over the last several years.

The first hour of the journey was a dense confusion of chatter, bellowing questions, profanities, and nerve-shattering noise from the male inmates. Their high spirits subsided when a shotgun-toting deputy racked a round in the chamber of his weapon. Valerie moved closer to the window and hoped to become as small a target as possible in case the deputy was the sort of man who could be capable of keeping the awful promise of his pointed threat. As the white security-transport bus rolled through the wooded countryside,

Valerie was grateful for the silence that finally descended.

The courtroom had been full to brimming. Friends of detainees, bonded misdemeanants, and felons sat in anxious clusters with their families and friends. Defense attorneys huddled near the judge's bench with court reporters and disinterested bailiffs. Valerie and four other defendants who had not been able to post bail or who had refused bail were flanked by wary deputies and brought into the court. They were paraded in their bright orange jail costumes before the suddenly hushed observers. The issued uniforms, handcuffs, and chains were a sharp contrast to the general attire of the room.

She did not know anyone. No one could help her make bail. It hadn't mattered. She was guilty. She had pled a week earlier hoping that her honesty and forthrightness would earn her the judge's compassion. Unlike her shackled partners, Valerie was there for sentencing.

Valerie's face flushed as the curious eyes of the room fell on her and her companions. She had little time for cause and concern however, as the chief bailiff directed the room's attention to the business of the day.

"Oyez, Oyez," he musically trumpeted. "All rise. The Honorable Judge Jonathan Simmons, District Court of Jackson, State of Missouri, is presiding this day." The chief bailiff's eyes quickly scanned the room for any who would dare to remain seated as the large, balding, and black-robed man briskly walked to the

raised bench. The bailiff hesitated a spare second after
the judge sat down before announcing, "Be seated."


The woods and brush beyond her window rushed
by in a blur. Like her life. With the miles falling away
below her feet, she had no sense of what lay ahead.
Someone else was driving. The controls were external,
not part of her, and not her choice. Her attorney had
been confident her guilty plea could help her. But the
judge surprised them. He had not agreed.


When it was finally Valerie's turn to stand before
the judge he looked at her over glasses set near the
tip of his nose and he clasped his hands in front of
his chest. "Do you remember what you pled last week,
Miss Blake?"

"Yes, I do," Valerie barely whispered. She coughed
to clear her throat. "Yes, I do, Your Honor," she
asserted cautiously.

"Has your attorney instructed you regarding the
structure of the presentence investigation report
conducted by the Jackson County probation office?"

"He has."

"Good. Then be informed," Judge Simmons intoned
as he flipped open the pages of the report and nodded
to the court reporter. "It is the determination of this
court that we accept your plea, and sentence you to
the minimum for felony driving under the influence.
Specifically, six months in the county jail and a
five-hundred-dollar fine."

Valerie blanched, her mouth fell open, and she turned toward her court-appointed attorney in protest. "I didn't know —" she stammered.

"Did not know what, Miss Blake?" the judge inquired.

"I . . . I didn't know what I was doing. I mean, I was drunk, I was driving the car. I admit that. But . . . I didn't know I'd go to jail. I thought there would be a choice . . . like treatment. Not just jail."

"It is always a matter of choice, young lady," he intoned at her from the high bench. "You're twenty-seven years old. That makes you an adult and responsible for your actions. More important to me, is the fact that this is the third time you've appeared before me in almost as many months," he said, flipping open the manila file folder in front of him. He moved his half-glasses down to the end of his nose and silently read the entries from the journal. Slowly, his lips compressed and turned down at the corners.

"Your Honor —" the lanky, court-appointed attorney at Valerie's side had tried to speak. He felt betrayed. He provided information and causal issues to the probation officer who had created the pre-sentence report. He had understood that the report would reflect Valerie Blake's victim status and would show that she needed more help than punishment.

"In a minute, counsel," Judge Simmons had growled.

"Miss Blake," the judge continued. "The first time I saw you was for public drunkenness. We saw fit at that time to release you on your promise to go for outpatient treatment. Two weeks later, after you had

voluntarily quit treatment before completion, you were
arrested for driving under the influence. At that point
the court in its mercy assigned you to probation for a
year, and thirty days' inpatient rehabilitation therapy
without imposition of a fine.

"You stand before me today, after pleading guilty to
a second driving-under-the-influence offense. I have
read the probation officer's report. I am familiar with
the fact that you are originally from Wyoming, and
your problems and difficulties in life. I fully realize
the pain and suffering that was your lot as a child
and young woman. However . . ." Judge Simmons took
off his glasses and rubbed at his weary eyes. "However, as difficult as your family life with your parents
may have been, and as overwhelming as your heritage
of alcohol consumption may be, and as understandable
as your desire for self-medicating to escape memories
of abuse may be, the law does not allow you to
continue to endanger yourself or others. It cannot. I
cannot. I have run the length of my sympathy, my
patience, and my ability to continue to let you attempt
to cooperatively work out your issues."

"If I could just have a moment, Your Honor,"
Valerie's court-appointed counsel began again in
desperation. He looked at the still woman in orange
standing beside him. He wanted to tell her how sorry
he was for misinterpreting the situation and for
misleading her. She was paying no attention to him.
Her gaze was fixed on the judge.

Valerie had mentally left the room. Only her body
remained standing before the bench. The terror of
imprisonment, the finality of the imposed sentence had

propelled her into a stunned silence. Her vision swirled before her, and everything receded into a darkening, sound-muffled tunnel.

"Not now," Judge Simmons said, silencing the recent bar graduate. He redirected his gaze to Valerie. "You have six months to work your problems through in Kansas City, Missouri, and more specifically, the Jackson County Jail. Excellent facilitators are available there for your recovery. I suggest you take full and complete advantage of the substance-abuse classes, counseling, and treatment the confinement offers. After that, if Missouri, and I dare say any other state, finds you guilty of driving under the influence, a two-to-three-year prison sentence will be next."

"Six months?" Valerie whispered in astonishment under her breath. Her large, brown eyes smarted, and she fought to keep her tears in check.

"Have I made myself clear?" he asked as he fairly leaned over the wide bench at her.

"Yes, Your Honor," Valerie and the appointed counsel had responded together.

"Good," the judge said, turning to the court recorder. "In the case of Jackson County, Missouri, versus Valerie Blake, conviction is upheld and sentence will be imposed. The sentence is for six months in the Jackson County Jail, to begin immediately. Dismissed," he said as he waved for the bailiff to take Valerie in custody.

The bailiff grabbed Valerie by the arm and pulled her toward the holding cell outside the courtroom. Valerie looked back in dismay. Neither the court-appointed counsel nor judge glanced at her as she was taken from the courtroom.

* * * * *

The passing greenery came back into focus in front of her eyes, and the reality of the hard bus bench reaffirmed it presence under her. She understood what the judge had been talking about, understood why he had made his decision, but that did nothing to help her understand what was happening to her now. Every minute of time she spent on the bus was taking her farther and farther from the treatment and counseling that had been available at the jail.

"Shit," she murmured heavily.

"That's no way for a pretty girl to talk."

Valerie glanced up to see the deputy who had threatened the bus passengers standing near her cage. The motion of the bus caused him to have to plant his feet wide on the metal floor and balance his posture by rocking on his toes. His mouth revealed a slight grin, but his eyes weren't smiling.

"Just thinking, boss," Valerie responded flatly.

"About what?"

"What's going on? Why am I on this bus? Where are we going, and why?"

"Didn't first shift at the jail tell you?"

"No one told me anything. I've been kidnaped and there's no ransom note," she joked, hoping he would offer information.

"Now that's funny. 'Jackson County sheriff's department kidnaps inmates to send them to new home.' " He chuckled.

"New home?"

"Yeah, you and the rest of this load are going to a new home."

"Where is our new home?" Valerie asked, trying to banter in her best respectful manner.

"Oh, it is not a matter of one new home. You're not going to the same place as those guys," the deputy said, nodding his head to the passengers at the rear. "We've got three stops to make before the end of the line. You'll be the last one we put off before we can turn this rig around and head back to Kansas City."

"Put off? Put off where?"

"Why, you're going to be the guest of some tiny town jail. Like these guys, but a bit deeper in the woods." He chuckled at her, showing tobacco-stained teeth.

"Do you think you could be any more obscure?"

"Watch it, girl." The deputy's eyes narrowed on her. "Its not my fault someone screwed up at the jail back there and forgot to tell you where you were headed and why. Just to set the record straight, you are not part of the need-to-know group. It's not like we're going to tell you anything about what we intend to do with you or anyone else at the jail. Hell, girl, what do you think we want to do? Set ourselves up for a jailbreak or something?"

"I just meant . . ."

"Apology accepted."

Valerie took a long, slow, deep breath and forced a smile across her lips. She wanted information, and a little from the deputy would make her feel better than none. "Right. It's just that I'm supposed to see my treatment counselor today. She won't know where I am, and the judge was really specific about me getting sober and staying that way."

10

"Ha. That's rich. Doesn't matter, though, one way or another now. You've been farmed out. You know, shit happens."

"What kinda shi— stuff happens. What happened?"

"There's no room at the inn, darlin'. That's what happened. You and the rest of this lot have been traded out for players to be named later. Some serious players are going to be taking your place. Jackson County Jail was about to get a bit too full again. Every time that happens, we have to shift out folks to the hinterlands," he commented. "Can't have overcrowding. 'Sides, you might not like whatever woman might be your bunkie."

"The jail's full?" She blinked. The idea of a jail getting full had never crossed her mind. She had never wondered what a jail would do if it did fill up.

"Sure is. Business is booming, you might say."

"You take inmates to other jails in Missouri?"

He crouched down near her cage and winked at her. "We don't just ship anyone. We only let these little cities and counties take care of our petty problems. Like you and this bunch. See, thing is, sometimes we get a full load of you folks, then sometimes all kinds of really big or bad things happen. Drunks, smalltime hoods, prostitutes, and misdemeanants are a dime a dozen. But murderers, major drug dealers, and other serious offenders need all the security our jail offers. So we ship the small shit out. Nothing or no one that would ever be a big problem for the small jails."

"I'm supposed to be in treatment," Valerie repeated. She wanted to see her counselor.

"Well," the deputy, said rising to his feet again, "that was then and this is now. You'll be lucky to have a comfortable bed out here in the sticks. I'm pretty sure the idea of providing any kind of treatment outside of three meals a day is a bit of a stretch for these folks. Understand?"

"No, I don't. I don't do this for a living. You do."

"Really?" The deputy picked up his clipboard and glanced through the sheets of paper. "Your rap sheet here says different. It says that you're here with us for good reason."

"Things were rough. I, I've made some mistakes."

"Well, then, this is another one. Think of it as your own special tour of central Missouri. You and these guys will get to spend the rest of your sentences from Jackson County as guests of little jails who like to earn some of their general operations funding by housing petty inmates when we've got bigger fish to fry."

"Petty?"

"Yeah. Not dangerous to no one, other than themselves. Bottom of the barrel."

The next half hour of the ride was interrupted only by the squeaking of seat springs and the shifting of the bus gears. The bus slowed on the outskirts of a small town and began a slow meandering through the streets before finally turning down an alley at the back of a small sheriff's department building. At the back of the building a portal entrance with bars and Plexiglas jutted out into the wide alley. The bus stopped at the portal door.

Valerie looked inside her paper sack of food and pulled out one of the three fried-egg sandwiches she'd been given. She watched the transfer take place as she ate.

The deputy and driver walked back to the end of the bus, unlocked the seat cuffs of three male inmates, and marched them out of the bus. Two local jailers in brown khaki uniforms and caps met the assembly at the door. The inmates were frisked while the Jackson County transport team watched. Papers were signed and exchanged before the inmates were directed to move inside. The deputy and driver got back into the bus. Fifteen minutes and another fried-egg sandwich later, the transport bus was out of town, heading for the next drop-off point.

"How much farther, boss?" Valerie asked as the deputy walked past her cage.

"Why?" You in a hurry?"

"No. Just wondering where I'll be having lunch," Valerie said, lying. She wanted a drink, maybe several. The unsettling change was making her nervous. A cold beer or two followed by a shot or three of bourbon was something she knew would settle her nerves. The idea of drinking, or of wanting or needing alcohol, was something she had managed to keep at bay for weeks. The need made her mouth water now, and there was nowhere to turn for comfort.

"Lunch, huh? You might as well sit back and relax. We drop off the rest of these guys first. Two or three more places. You're last on our list. At the rate we're going and the distance we have to travel, I'd say you'll be getting lunch sometime after five this evening."

"But, you said —"

"I didn't make any promises. Simply guessing. Every jail's different, and the next two have a whole lot of preparation, processing, and paperwork for us before it's called done," he said, glancing at the opened paper bag on the seat next to Valerie. "If I was you, I'd go real slow on whatever you got left in there. See, the jails will feed the driver and me, but all you got between here and your new home is what's in that bag. Trust me, we're not making any runs through a fast-food drive-in. Didn't your daddy ever teach you to plan ahead?"

"What he taught me is none of your fucking business," Valerie snapped back in anger.

"Whoa, I hit a nerve or something. What happened to you saying Boss this, and Boss that?"

"Just leave my father out of this."

"You're touchy all right. You worried he wouldn't be happy to see his little girl riding in a jail-transport vehicle? Don't tell me now, drunks don't run in your family? It's a problem that you acquired all on your own?" the deputy teased.

"Fuck him and fuck you!" Valerie shouted as she tried to rise from the seat as far as her chains would allow.

The deputy raised his hand at her as though he might strike her through the steel mesh of the cage. He bared his teeth and turned away from her to return to the front of the bus. Valerie seethed in anger as she watched the man's head bob in conversation while he spoke to the driver. Her father was the last person in the world Valerie wanted to think about. She didn't want to remember him, his face, his hands, his smell. There was nothing to think about so far as she was concerned. Nothing was worth remembering, and everything was worth forgetting.

# Chapter 2

Valerie was the only prisoner remaining on the bus. The hours and miles had begun to seem interminable. The transport unit had made a total of seven stops. Rarely did more than one prisoner get escorted into any of the small jails along the route. Even for Missouri the tiny communities that boasted a county seat seemed cold, dreary, and colorless. The brilliant autumn leaves had vanished over a month ago. November lay across the rolling bluffs, naked trees, and sparsely sprinkled evergreens as a prelude to winter.

She had begun to think the thinly padded seat to which she was shackled would wear holes through her flesh where the bones of her hips met the unyielding metal. Her sole pleasure came from the slowly decreasing level of noise from the steadily declining number of males remaining on the bus. There were fewer farts drifting through the air, fewer taunts directed toward her, and fewer eyes boring into the back of her neck.

Waiting for the transfer while sitting in the bus had been difficult to endure. There was no circulating heat. Valerie's loose-fitting jumpsuit seemed to let the cool air drift over her T-shirt and blow chillingly around her waist. She had no watch, but she calculated that each off-loading consumed a half hour or more. Long enough for her toes to feel the coldness of the steel floor begin to creep up her legs. The gray rain clouds and overcast sky combined to depress her mood and chill her only a little more than her predicament.

The bus shifted to a lower gear as the pavement widened. The twists and turns on the two-lane blacktop seemed to spread out to reveal yet another small town hiding in the thick woods. Valerie wondered if they were still in Missouri.

"Well, looks like we've made it to your new home," the armed deputy remarked.

As Valerie looked out of the window in a mixture of relief and apprehension, the bus bounced along the cobblestone street. She could hear the gears grinding lower as the bus lumbered toward a squat, native-stone building.

"It's puny." She breathed and fogged the chilled air on the window.

"No more than they need, trust me," the armed deputy said as he stood.

From her window through the drizzle of rain, Valerie could see the building hunkered against a backdrop of parklike planted trees. Yellow and fluorescent office lights twinkled in the darkening gloom of the day. Attached to the north end of the sheriff's office and jail was what looked like an over-sized garage made of wood and steel. The transport bus pulled down the asphalt drive toward the huge garage, and the large steel door rolled up. The bright interior revealed a second giant garage door at the opposite end. Two male deputies stood near the wall and waited for the transport bus to come to a halt inside the sally port. One deputy waved to the driver indicating a red line in front of the rear door and signaled him to cut his engine.

The transport-deputies left Valerie on the bus while they chatted animatedly with their local counterparts. Short moments later, the armed transport-deputy returned to the bus, unlocked Valerie's tiny cell door, and released the check-chain that had attached her leg-irons to the floor of the bus.

"This is where you get off," he said as he grabbed her arm. He held on to help her waddle down the aisle, take the steps down, and half jump out into the glare of the sally port. The driver handed a clipboard with a file over to the deputy nearest Valerie.

"The paperwork," he said, and nodded to Valerie.

"She got any stuff . . . personal items or other effects?" the blue-shirted local asked.

"A box in the lockbox. You want to search it first and then her?" the transport-driver responded.

"We'll check the box out here to make sure it's all accounted for," the local grinned. "You think she was able to conceal any shotguns or bayonets after you put her on the bus?" he said, winking.

The four deputies turned to look at Valerie standing in the oversized orange jumpsuit and jailhouse slippers. Their sudden burst of laughter was startling in the steel-sided echo chamber of the spacious sally port. The short, round deputy chucked his taller partner on the arm and walked toward the bus. He returned in a few moments with a twenty-four-inch square cardboard box that held all of Valerie Blake's personal belongings.

"This would be it, Sam," the rotund deputy said as he jerked his head at Valerie. "Take her to the holding cell. I'll get the cook to get these guys some food, and then we can finish checking her in," he said as he walked toward the flat-barred door leading into the interior of the jail.

"Want me to put her in lockup or the cell?" the older deputy asked.

"Just put her in lockup for right now. Plenty of time 'til we sort these things out and finish the paperwork."

The older deputy took Valerie by the arm. "This way," he directed.

The holding cell was small, an eight-by-six room void of bed, chair, window, and comfort. There was a toilet. Valerie's eyes locked on it immediately.

"Deputy?" Valerie said as she hobbled into the cell.

"Yes'm," the deputy replied in courteous, old-fashioned Southern habit.

"Deputy . . . sir . . ." Valerie said, picking up on his suggestion of civility. "I have to go to the bathroom. Real bad." She turned toward him and held her shackled hands toward him. "Could you . . . would you? Please?"

"Well . . . it's a bit unusual, seeing as how we haven't checked you in and all."

"Yes, but if I were a man, I wouldn't have to ask you to help make it possible for me to use that toilet. I need to take this thing off," she said, shrugging in her clothes.

He looked at her, and a sudden dawning of her predicament spread over his face. "I suppose that's right. See here that you don't go causing any mischief 'cause I helped you," he warned as he unlocked the handcuffs, the belly-chain, and the shackles at her feet.

The iron-and-steel bindings dropped to the floor. The deputy quickly reached down and snatched them away from her. "You cause any problems for me, and I promise that the next four months will be the longest of your life," he said as he moved out of the room and locked the door. The heavy steel door clanged shut.

"No problem. You have my word," Valerie promised.

Valerie tore at the snaps on the jumpsuit and almost leaped at the brushed aluminum commode sitting promisingly in a corner of her tiny cell.

Relief was almost orgasmic.


Over the next two hours an occasional unsmiling face of a uniformed officer would momentarily pop into view at the window. The furrowed brows and unspeaking eyes were all the company she had while she sat and waited on the cement floor. "Frying pan to fire," she muttered haplessly.

Then, unexpectedly, she heard the rattle of keys in the door. "Sorry about the wait, young lady," a middle-aged, thickset uniformed officer said as he opened the door. "Shift change and all the confounding confusion that goes with it," he added as he motioned for her to follow him.

"I thought maybe you forgot me," she said in casual conversation as he waved her in front of him.

"Not hardly. Be hard to forget a commodity."

"Commodity?" Valerie asked as he touched her right shoulder and guided her toward what appeared to be the jail's receiving area.

An ancient battery of recycled metal military desks hugged the walls. Several chairs were placed near the desks and an Instamatic camera stood mounted on a tripod near a corner grouping of long mirrors at the back. The deputy took her elbow and glided her toward the mirrors.

"Yeah. At sixty-seven dollars a day, you more than pay for your keep," he stated. "Now, just stand in front of those mirrors, hold this plaque, and say *cheese*," he directed as he moved Valerie in front of the camera.

She saw her name on the booking plaque, the day's date, and her new inmate number. In bold print under the personal information was the name of her home for the next four months, CHIMNEY ROCK JAIL. She looked up in time to be blinded by the quick strobe of light from the camera.

"I can't pay sixty-seven dollars a day," she protested aloud.

The deputy snorted and then guffawed. "Not you, young lady. The Jackson County Jail and the good people of Kansas City, Missouri, are footing the bill," he explained.

"Oh?"

"Go sit over there at the desk where I have the computer," he directed as he chuckled again to himself. "That's rich. Gotta remember to tell the wife," he said as he shook his head at the floor.

"I don't mean to be stupid," Valerie tried to explain.

"That's fine. The idea hit my funny bone. Maybe it's something we can start here. Might keep a few more people honest or sober. What do you think?"

"Can't say I understand why you would keep other people's prisoners."

"It's easy. The more of you Kansas City folks we hold, the more money we make. We got ourselves five cells here. No waiting. The whole idea's pretty easy. How's your math?" he asked as he sat down behind the computer and pulled out a manila file with the name VALERIE BLAKE written in bold magic marker across the face.

"There's a test?" Valerie asked in bewilderment.

"Ha," he laughed. "You're a card, aren't you?"

With growing concern, she eyed her jailer skeptically. He was making it hard to get her bearings, and it had been an overwhelmingly confusing day. She wasn't trying to be funny. She simply did not know the rules everyone else was playing by. Her new home was more confusing than the jailer's words.

The peeling paint, battered wood trim, reject furniture, odd computer, and general unkempt appearance of the processing room were absurd to her. She had grown used to the spit and polish of the Jackson County Jail. There, the county employees and trustee inmates worked in seemingly fevered pace to maintain a clean, sanitary, and safe environment. She knew. She'd spent more than one night in cheap motels that would not have passed the rigorous inspections held at the Jackson County Jail. The jailers there were firm but not impolite. They maintained order of everything and discipline of everyone. Their uniforms were starched and pressed.

The deputy sitting at the desk now was another exception to the regimentation her two months at Jackson County had taught her. He was a large, soft-looking man with a shock of unruly thick, brown hair. His tan, sun-scored face, neck, arms, and hands were oddly offset by the hint of pale skin peeking around the corners of his shirt neck and sleeves. He had large hands with nothing soft about them. His hands were those of a man who knew about hard work, hard labor, and making ends meet on a daily basis. His thick, flesh-ringed neck betrayed day-old perspiration and a minor accumulation of dirt in the creases. He had the look of a man who worked two jobs in order to keep hearth and home together. She glanced at his name tag.

"Mr. Dawes?"

"Yeah?" Deputy Dawes said, looking up from the manila folder.

"I haven't eaten since around noon. Is there any chance of getting some food?"

"You mean those two didn't feed you?"

"No, sir."

"Well, doesn't that just beat all," Dawes said, shaking his head in disbelief. "Tell you what, when we get finished here I'll rustle something up for you. Deal?" he asked.

"Deal," Valerie quickly agreed.

"OK. Let's do this right and quick. Full name. Last, middle, and then first. Date of birth, place of birth, height, weight, and the rest," Dawes said, studying the computer-generated form in front of him.

"Blake, B-L-A-K-E, I don't have a middle name, but the first is Valerie. Do you want me to spell it?"

"No need. Like it sounds, isn't it?"

"Yes. I was born May 15, 1971, Blue Springs, Wyoming. Last time I checked I was five feet six, one hundred twenty-five pounds, brown hair, and brown eyes."

"Kinda thin, aren't you?" Dawes asked as he eyed her.

"That has been part of my trouble. Been drinking too much and not eating regular. I was working out in the gym at the jail and eating a lot of starchy food. But I was only in that program a month, not enough time to get back what I've lost."

"You'll eat pretty good around here. We may not look like much, but the food is good and plenty. All right now, home address, next of kin, and any medical problems we should know about," Dawes said as he finished the first part of the form.

"None, none, and none," Valerie whispered.

Jailer Dawes's head whipped from his concentration on the computer monitor and looked intently at his prisoner. "None?"

23

"None. Not a thing. And nothing I care to re-member."

A fleeting grimace pulled at the corners of Dawes's lips as he turned his eyes back to his form. He cleared his throat. "So they didn't feed you, huh?" It was subterfuge, a way to clear his head from thinking about how hard some people seemed to have life. He'd transported prisoners before. None of those in his care ever went without eating. It rankled him how some people never understood the little things. They went through life never guessing that there but for the grace of God, went one and all. Dawes knew, and he knew from personal experience. A misstep here, a slip there, and a bit of loneliness and misdirection too big to recover from could send most folks slipping over the edge. His life had led him to believe that in some instances there was little more than the width of the desk between him and the circumstances of those he booked into the jail.

"It will take a few more minutes here and getting you fingerprinted before I can find something for you. That'll work, won't it?"

"That would be super," Valerie responded, sensing a shift in his mood.

"Only right," Dawes muttered under his breath.

Fifteen minutes after the completion of the intake process, Valerie was escorted to the single bunked room at the end of a short hallway. She carried two toasted-cheese sandwiches, a saucer with two large pieces of apple pie, and a plastic thermos of coffee. She carefully balanced her food all the way to her cell and stood expectantly at the door.

Her cell was located a few feet south, opposite a set of large, barred doors. On the facing side of the cell she saw an open shower room and padlocked storage door. Through the barred doors she could hear the distant rumbling sounds of male voices. She was grateful for the slight buffering and damping of noise provided by the length of the opposite block of cells.

Dawes opened the barred door and held it for her. "You eat all you want. I'll be back in ten minutes to get that thermos from you. I got to get back up to the front. It's my turn on the dispatch radio tonight and I'd bet the road-deputy is dying of boredom up there. You know, I shouldn't let you have that stuff in your cell like that, but I don't imagine you'd be able to hang yourself with it. Y'all think?" He grinned at her as he shut and locked the heavy door.

Valerie walked over to the tiny desk, set her food down on the little tabletop, and hurriedly pulled the chair over. The first thing she did was unwrap one of the plastic-covered pieces of pie and shove it into her mouth. It was ambrosia.

"Hmmm." She chewed appreciatively. The thick, sweet juices of apple slid down her throat. Her taste buds were in heaven. Every morsel tasted amazing. The coffee was black, hot, and warming. She gulped and choked. Coughing, she tried to still herself and eat more slowly. She wanted to taste everything, to let it fill her up. She tried not to worry that her jailer might change his mind and come back for the bounty he had given her.

By six-thirty the next morning John Dawes was in his truck driving out of town toward his farm and home. He hummed to himself, thinking about the hotcakes, eggs, and bacon his wife would be preparing for breakfast. The mornings were theirs alone. With the children on the school bus by the time he turned into the driveway, he and his wife, Harriet, would be able to eat and talk before she had to leave for her nursing job at the Chimney Rock County Hospital.

That time of sharing had become important to them. There was so little time to relax and share anymore. Four years before, neither one of them would have believed that his part-time job at the sheriff's department would become a full-time necessity. They had hoped that the farm would do better, become more prosperous, become less of a burden. They still managed to dream that it would recover and begin to show some real profit again.

Reality intruded on his thoughts as he recalled how Harriet had intended the same type of short-term solution when she went back to work at the hospital. Two years ago, she had taken some night courses, gotten recertified, and begun supplementing the family's income. Then, as things have a way of doing, the short solution became a way of life. The children kept growing and needing things like clothes, shoes, and schoolbooks. The farm earnings varied and, try as they could, hanging on was the best they could manage.

Through it all, they felt luckier than most. They still had the farm. The same could not be said of everyone whose small farm who had once dotted the county. John and Harriet had not yet been forced by bank or tax auction to move away from their beloved green rolling hills in the Ozarks.

John Dawes was beginning to believe that the longer he was with the sheriff's department, the greater the likelihood he had of retiring from the job. He was fine with the idea. The farm had been in the family for three generations, and he was determined not to lose it. The long hours in the fields were not enough to make him want to leave. Harriet agreed. The Ozarks offered them everything they had ever wanted, like clean air, clean water, and room to feel free.

John tried to shake off his concerns. As he pulled up to the house, he looked across the wide field behind and began making a list of things he wanted to get done that day. He intended to set about his chores the moment his wife left for work. He would try to catch a few winks before his shift began at the jail that evening.

Harriet opened the back door to the kitchen as he walked up the wooden steps. Her bright eyes and loving smile lightened his heart. The wide smile he offered back to her reflected his love for her. Things could be worse, he thought, as his mind returned briefly on the sad face of the young woman who was to be a full-time guest at the jail for the next four months. Things could also get better if one stayed the course. He prayed silently for any and all in need.

# Chapter 3

Detective Tru North ran the fingers of her right hand through her auburn hair in frustration. Lieutenant Haines was talking about taking her from her regular duties in the homicide division and loaning her out, without her partner, to the newly created metro-squad homicide coalition. Try as she might, she could not make sense of his insistence that she join the coalition as a representative of the Kansas City, Missouri, homicide division. She did not want the assignment. She did not see herself as needing any more contacts with FBI agents or other regionally assigned officers. She was not looking for a promotion or an enhancement of her internal political career. Her assurance and personal sense of the familiar had been shaken during the month of October. It was unnerving to believe that she would be on dubious professional ground as well.

A relatively new transfer from operations planning, and recently returned from the FBI Academy, Lieutenant Haines seemed insistent and genuinely excited about Tru's experiencing team serial-homicide investigation. His six-foot-three-inch, two-hundred-fifty-two-pound frame seemed at odd opposition to his the persuasive tones and body language. He had not ordered her to join the coalition. Instead of rankling at her reluctance, as his predecessor might have done, he had changed tactics. Over the course of the last twenty minutes, Tru had been amazed at his discourse on the skills in team investigating that she would develop. Additionally, he pointed out the singular importance of bringing the Blue River Stalker to justice.

Detective Tru North felt her jaw drop slightly. Recovering, she managed to ask a question over the lieutenant's continuing verbal exposition. "So this isn't just an assignment for general purposes? It's not a training exercise? You want me to work on this team thing because they are focusing on the Blue River Stalker?" The heat of excitement flushed her face.

Lieutenant Haines grinned at her sudden comprehension. "Absolutely. Detective, here's the deal," he said, clearing his throat. "As it currently stands, you are one of the youngest members on our squad, and I've been going through your service record," he said as he picked up a folder with Tru's name on it.

Tru felt the hair on the back of her neck rise. Her history with the homicide unit had been one long succession of less-than-amusing experiences with many of her supervisors. The past six months had been fairly tranquil when compared to previous cycles in her life, and she did not wish to be engaged in supervision-by-combat. She felt reasonably confident regarding the contents of her personnel service record, but she knew there was an off chance that a detraction or two might have made its way into the file without her knowledge. The file in the lieutenant's hands was not the official file; it was the working file. Her heart skipped a beat.

"I see here," Lieutenant Haines began again when he had located what he had been searching for in the folder, "these notes indicate that you have had quite a bit of success as a homicide investigator, albeit some luck and a tendency for unconventional techniques appear to be your hallmark. I think that this shows that you have great promise. Even with that," he said, flipping to the front of the folder, "it would appear that, for whatever reason, you haven't been given many of the same opportunities for training that most of the other members of this squad have enjoyed." He set the folder on the desk between them and eyed his young detective with a mixture of interest and curiosity.

"Don't you find that odd, detective?"

Tru was grateful that no breeze could blow in through the closed windows behind the lieutenant and that no overhead fans were turned on, because she was sure that the slightest gust would have knocked her out of her chair.

"Odd?" Tru managed to croak as she struggled to keep what felt like a very silly grin from spreading across her face.

"Certainly odd in my opinion. You have managed to be fairly creative in bringing a number of individuals to trial and securing their convictions. Furthermore, it would appear that when necessary you've also managed to finish off a few, thereby saving the citizens and the system a great deal of expense. Mind you, it's not exactly what we want to have happen unless absolutely necessary. Then again, when you did, they were good, righteous shoots."

"Your point would be, lieutenant?" Tru asked carefully and began looking around for the cameras she was sure he had hidden in the room. She waited for some of her cohorts to rush into the room and announce the name of the game they were playing on her.

Tru had no direct experience of appreciation from a supervisor who sounded like he cared about her professional life or actually knew about any skills she had obtained by accident or hard-won discipline. She had spent years in law enforcement, slowly but surely gaining begrudging acceptance and respect from the majority of her peers and superiors.

Her tendency for aloofness had not helped her develop more than a handful of friends. The aloofness was her protective coloration, a way of keeping her life and interests personal. Tru shared little of herself and rarely asked more of others. This behavior extended past her professional demeanor and into her personal lifestyle. She didn't keep others from sharing; rather, she didn't intend to be reciprocal. Bells, which could warn her against the potential for betrayal, suddenly set up an incredible din inside her head.

"The point would be, Detective North, that I intend to see to it that you begin to get some of those opportunities. It doesn't do this unit, or me as your supervisor, any good to fail to see that you get the training and the opportunities necessary to make you more successful as an investigator."

"That is very generous of you, lieutenant," Tru said slowly.

"It's not generosity," Haines asserted. "It's a fact. There is organization and self-interest on my part.

"I don't know what difficulties you may have had with your supervisors in the past, and I don't care. Those things have been dealt with and resolved. They're history. I'm the new kid on the block, and as of now it's a new day and a new way. Your history begins, here and with me," he said as he leaned back in his chair.

"I'm not quite sure I understand completely."

"Or *believe,* if I read the tone of your voice correctly," he said, as he let a hint of a grin flicker across his face. "It does not matter. In time you will understand and maybe even begin to believe that I do not have a hidden agenda with you or anyone in this department. The why of it? It's my style. The truth of it? Well, that may be something for you to learn," he said as he tossed the file with her name on it in the trash basket near his desk.

"I see."

"You will. But getting back to your assignment, the one I hope you'll be taking. I want you to join the metro-regional task force charged with the identification and apprehension of the Blue River Stalker. Are you interested?"

A hundred thoughts ran through her head. She took a deep breath before allowing her interest to leap into the proffered unknown.

"Yes, I am interested." The habitual voice of caution mumbled at the back of her mind.

"Splendid. Here," he said, as he took a folded piece of paper from his right breast pocket and held it out. "Report to this man tomorrow at that address. He'll be expecting you."

"You were confident I would say yes?" Tru asked, gingerly taking the card from his hand and wondering how much she had underestimated him.

"No, detective. I did not know you would agree. But I had my hopes. Think of it as a calculated risk. I read that working file, the one I'll shred. Everything in there told me that given a fair shake, you could rise to any challenge that might come your way. That's what this is, detective. It's an opportunity and a challenge that I believe you can meet."

"I see. Thank you," Tru said. She rose from the chair. As she turned to leave the lieutenant's office, she felt a dual sense of elation and apprehension.

"By the way, detective . . ."

"Yes, sir?"

"There's a fresh body."

"When?"

"Last night. By the looks of it, the killer may have claimed his seventh victim. But I'm sure they'll get you up to speed on that when you arrive. Good luck."

"Thank you, sir."

\* \* \* \* \*

Haines finished shredding the working file and reached for his phone. He could hear the soft, purring ring of the phone in his ear as he waited for someone to answer.

"Hello?" The phone was answered with a firm, smooth inquiry.

"How is my favorite aunt?" Haines asked cheerfully.

"Absolutely fine, 'cause I don't sit in my house and wait by the phone for my relatives to call. Where have you and your family been? And how's that sister of mine?" the woman requested firmly.

"One, it's a long story and two, Mom is fine. She told me to send you her love and to tell you that she expects to be home in mid-March. I had several reasons to call, however. Sara and I would love to have you come over for dinner on Friday night. It would be a good time for me to bring you up to speed about one of your former pupils."

"A former pupil?"

"And friend, a certain Detective North."

"What has happened now?"

"Nothing, Mary Margaret. I simply thought you would like to know she has a new supervisor," he said, grinning into the phone.

"And who the hell would that be?" retired police department Major O'Donoghue asked.

"Why, your favorite nephew, of course. Didn't Mom tell you I got that promotion?"

"Your mother, dear boy, only remembers what her last golf score was when she's snowbirding it down in New Mexico. So you're the new head honcho in homicide?" Major O'Donoghue said, beaming with pride.

34

"That I am, and Ms. Tru North and I were just talking. She's an interesting piece of work. Might be a challenge to supervise, if I remember correctly some of the things you've told me over the years."

"Piece of work?" Major O'Donoghue rankled. "I'll have you know she's a good girl — and probably one of the better detectives you have up there," she responded irritably. Tru had been one of her favorite students before O'Donoghue retired from the University of Missouri at Kansas City. During those last two years, she found Tru to be one of the most sincere and earnest students she had had during her whole tenure. That they became friends was natural. Both were headstrong, inquisitive, and assertively intelligent. After O'Donoghue's retirement, Tru kept in touch and occasionally visited her with conversation about house maintenance and problematic cases.

"Now simmer down. I didn't mean anything hurtful by the comment. Seems to me, you and she have a lot in common, like attitude and wariness. You've given me an apparently very accurate portrayal of her demeanor. Everything I've read about her in the department intimates that she is a fine investigator, although she has a tendency to irritate people once in a while. Personally, I think she's been overlooked for praise, performance, and promotion a bit too often, and I suspect some pretty big egos have been getting in her way. She's not perfect, mind you, not by a long shot, but then, no one is but you, dear lady."

"You're full of it this morning, aren't you?" O'Donoghue laughed. "Did you tell Tru what you think about her performance record ? Or did you keep that to yourself?"

"Mostly I kept it to myself. She doesn't know me from Adam, and I don't want you to enlighten her, either. She's quite capable of making it on her own, if given as much opportunity and recognition as the rest of the staff. I'm going to keep my eye on her, but no special privileges or anything like that," he asserted.

"Tru's not had much in the way of special privileges ever. If anything, just the opposite. Seems to me she wouldn't know how to handle too much that's positive. She hasn't had enough practice. She might be concerned about your motives. I would be," O'Donoghue chided.

"Not likely, Aunt Mary Margaret. Sara can still score higher on the firing range than I can. I'd have to be a damn big fool to risk losing Sara or to ignore the possible threat of her putting a hole in me to get my attention," he professed.

"I'm glad to hear it, for the unit in general and for Tru in particular. I'll take you up on that dinner. Give my love to Sara," O'Donoghue said.

"Great. It will be good to see you again. We have to get a bit more regular about this sort of thing, now that I'm in town again on a regular basis. And, we'll keep this thing about you and me being related between us, won't we?"

"I've been known to keep a secret or two in my time. I can manage this one. When you talk to your mother again, tell her to call me. I want to know what the Irish have to wear for skin protection in the sun-baked broiler country."

"Will do," Lieutenant Haines said. He heard the line go dead.

\* \* \* \* \*

Over the course of the following two weeks, Detective Tru North's days and nights were consumed by her involvement with the metro-regional task force. Special Agent Charles G. Douglas of the area FBI office had been placed in charge of the special unit. The first task he assigned Tru was to get up to speed on the investigative techniques the squad, under his command, was using to get a handle on the Blue River Stalker.

He handed her copies of thick case files, a stack of books, and copies of research articles related to serial homicide investigation and pointed her toward an empty desk. His directives were brief and to the point. He wanted her to take no active part in the investigative footwork until she was thoroughly steeped in her reading homework. He told her to read the tomes and research articles first and then and only then ... review the homicide investigation reports.

Tru was a bit stupefied at the briskness of his manner and the schoolgirl task he had given her. She wanted to bristle, to assert that she was a detective, not an apprentice to his investigative process and procedures. She felt the hackles going up on the back of her neck until she remembered Lieutenant Haines's real support for her work. Begrudgingly, she shrugged and accepted the directives from Agent Douglas.

Her tiny desk overflowed with files and books. Tru sat down and gazed about the room of milling task-force officers. As she scanned the room, she noticed two other desks piled high with files, papers, and books saw the bent heads of deputies frowning through their reading, furiously scribbling notes as they read. One deputy glanced up at her momentarily, shrugged, and returned to his investigative paper research.

As she watched the comings and goings of other detectives, a lanky male detective from North Kansas City, Missouri, hesitated by her desk. "It's his idea of educating the hicks," the detective grumbled at her. "He got his serial homicide investigation certificate six months ago. Damn proud of it, too. Figures he has to lead us by the hand before he can trust us out in the field. Asshole."

"Equal opportunity asshole," Tru snorted.

"Yeah. He sure does do it to everyone. Like some sort of initiation thing. By the way, at seven A.M. every Monday of the world he has a meeting. Don't miss it, and for godsake don't be late. He doesn't humiliate, but your supervisor will be informed of every move you make or don't make, which suits the bastard," the detective, said moving off to his desk.

"Gotcha," Tru said, nodding at her retreating information source. She looked at the stacks of readings and her copies of the homicide reports. *Not my ball and not my park*, she reminded herself, trying to adjust to the work harness the special agent seemed to have placed around her shoulders.

She reached for the first book and settled back in her chair, willing herself to go along with the program. In her heart and mind, she wanted to take advantage of the situation. She knew what it could mean . . . positive future with the KCMO homicide division. She had volunteered for this assignment, and it was her responsibility to work within the framework of that post.

Tru found the books, research articles, and case-file analysis interesting, if not a bit puzzling. The books were an analytic compilation of investigative procedures that had been developed by the FBI and its cohorts for cases involving serial murder. Some of the historic and leading names in the field of violent-crime investigation were contributors. There was a great deal of self-aggrandizing commentary by former and current behavioral science unit agents, but most of the stuff was interesting. Tru managed to wade through article after article taken from the *FBI Bulletin* and law enforcement journals. By the end of the second week she was sure that if she had to read the initials *FBI* again, she would scream.

Much of the reading was about courses and case materials that she had been independently reading over the last several years. She found it curious how the FBI had treated the same information she had researched. One of the main differences was the structured modeling and classification characteristic of the FBI format. There was a tendency to construct big overviews of profiled material without any inferences or explanations as to how or why the assumptions about the unknown murderers were drawn. It was frustrating.

Tru studiously constructed notes, figuring that even bad examples serve some greater purpose. The special agent, in his case analysis, contended that their serial rapist-murderer was performing "organized sexual homicides." Tru managed to garner that the suspect engaged in sexual activity with the victim. According to the special agent, the killer chose someone who fit his preferences, stalked his victim, prepared himself, and planned for the hunt and kill.

The reading and analysis was taking time. Too much time. But enough time for Tru to let her attention to her life beyond homicide investigation slip and slide. She was not earning points from either of the women who had captured her interest and her heart. The fact that there were two was a problem for Tru.

Tru had been forthcoming with arson investigator CB Belpre. CB was aware of Marki, but Marki had no knowledge of CB or of Tru's dalliance.

Ph.D. and psychologist Marki Campbell at the University of Missouri at Kansas City had no idea that the complexion of the relationship that she and Tru had developed over the last year had drastically changed with the appearance of CB Belpre. To make matters worse, Marki believed that they would solidify their relationship and formalize their love by committing to each other.

Tru had made no promises to either of them. She had maintained her apartment, her separateness, and her independence. She convinced herself that no commitment could or should be made to either, particularly Marki, who at every occasion insisted that she move in.

At thirty-two, Tru North had grown weary of rashly conceived liaisons. She had seen all that she ever wanted to. Marki's possessiveness alarmed her and reminded her of poorly bargained promises she had made in the past. She was firm in her decision not to go there again.

Tru's fear of commitment rose from memories. Some memories were from her childhood and youth. Other memories clustered around misplaced trusts. She was tired. She was weary of wanting and afraid of needing. She had vowed never to make a fool of anyone, especially herself, ever again.

There was no way she would allow her desires for a relationship, her erotic compulsion, and her intimate dreams to be faulted, abused, or annihilated by another's thoughtlessness or best intention. She courted, longed for, and loved Marki and CB as best she could.

The miracle of distance afforded by her attachment to the metro-regional squad aided her in eluding the promises and the crucial questions of lovers. The reckoning loomed ahead. And her uncertain heart held her captive.

# Chapter 4

"This is what I get for insisting," Detective Tru North intoned as she tossed another cigarette out the window of her unmarked patrol unit. She had volunteered, no, insisted on conducting the lone stakeout. She had campaigned in a persistent war of fraying nerves with the ever-weakening resistance of the task-force commander. Tru, utilizing her newly acquired information had asserted that a stakeout in the vicinity of a body-drop location could be fruitful to the investigation. The FBI agent, on the other hand, has asserted that her plan was too much of a long shot and a waste of precious investigative resources. In frustration, he had finally relented simply to get her out of his office. As one of the detectives assigned to the regional task force, Tru was anxious for the killer to give clues to his identity. She hoped they did not have to wait for another body to appear.

Feeling the damp night of November flow over her, she was beginning to believe that the FBI agent had been right about a stakeout being a waste of time. A week had gone by, and her efforts at the various locations had yielded no more and no less than the efforts of those who were doing other types of footwork in the special squad. She was no more impatient to capture the killer than her counterparts, and that was extreme. Even so, she was getting tired working all day and staying up most of the night.

In general in the greater Kansas City, Missouri, metropolitan area, the victims were considered a low priority by many of the citizens. Petty drug offenders and socially detached women with suspected or known histories of prostitution were not the sort to raise alarm in the suburbs. Their deaths along the gentle, lapping waters of the Big Blue barely raised an eyebrow in the safe homes along the quieter, more gracious streets. The task force members had interviewed all available family members of the deceased. Additionally, the task force had responded to the hundreds of investigative tips gleaned from the crime-information hot line. They had picked up and briefly held for interrogation known sex offenders living near the victims' residences and had staked out known pick-up areas nearby without results.

But Tru believed that the river had not given up all its secrets.

Tru could hear the distant whine of late-night traffic coursing along south I-70. She raised the night-vision goggles to her face and searched the rolling terrain for the man they had dubbed the Blue River Stalker. As the fifth night of her vigilance wore on, she could not shake the sinking feeling that she was engaged in a pointless long shot. Tru raised the last of the cooling cup of coffee to her lips and let the cold caffeine glide down her throat.

The month of November had been full of potential. Rain promised a wet and drizzling winter. Spring was a long way away. She vowed to take a vacation in May, if the FBI squad leader would let her have some time by then. She wanted time to think. The faces of Marki Campbell and CB Belpre swirled in front of her tired eyes. They were so different. Both had unique and wonderful qualities. Individually they held her heart for their own special reasons. Tangled as she was between them, she knew she was courting disaster.

Psychology professor Marki Campbell, the lovely woman with copper hair and green eyes, had steadily become a part of Tru's life during the past year. With Marki's quick mind, penetrating intellect, and full-bodied comfort, Tru found the security she never dreamed possible. Marki's intense, earnest, and probing compassion and passion for Tru's emotional needs left Tru reeling. Tru had literally fallen into her arms, maybe a bit too hard and too fast

As good as Marki's companionship was, Tru found herself chafing under Marki's tendency for professional scrutiny, her probing and disquieting insistence for questioning who, what, when, where, and why. Tru could not comfortably endure that sort of exploration.

There had been several arguments, not vicious but pointed. Finally, Marki's techniques began to wear holes in the relationship. And Tru balked at Marki's constant and subtle insistence that Tru commit herself to their relationship. After months of frequent demands, Tru had been weakening. Then everything changed when Tru met arson investigator CB Belpre.

At forty-two, CB Belpre was ten years Tru's senior. She had the wonderful traits of self-assurance, poise, and wry sense of humor. CB's presence and confidence had shaken Tru out of her mounting complacency. CB did not use emotional manipulation or skillfully assembled rationales. Tru loved to run her fingers through the emerging flecks of gray in CB's dark hair. She loved to run her hands along CB's lean, statuesque body and hear CB breathing peacefully near her in the night.

CB and Tru had engaged in a slow dance toward each other. During and after the heat of intimacy, CB and Tru shared conversations, contacts, work, and mutuality of interests.

It had been different with Marki; there the fire had almost consumed her the first night. The intensity had become an imposition of expectations from Marki. Tru loved Marki, but their relationship changed as Marki became possessive.

CB and Tru had a lot in common. They both liked to laugh, although CB saw the humor in life more quickly than Tru. And as an arson investigator, CB understood the investigative and law enforcement world in which Tru lived. There was no distrust because there was no commitment and no insistence on one. CB knew about Marki and tried never to push Tru to do more than what Tru was ready to do. CB appeared to understand that all personal decisions between them had to be mutual. Tru wondered if CB was the authentic complement for her heart and love, her gentle companion in life.

Tru sipped the last of the coffee and knew she would have to finally tell the truth to Marki before real damage was done. Tru stretched in resignation and irritation in the darkened car.

Suddenly, an abrupt movement along the narrow roadway caught her attention. The low, heavy shadow of a large American car eased its bulk toward the parkway on the river shore drive. The driver had turned his headlights off and was trying to drive by the thin light of the half moon. Tru heard the sound of scattered gravel being crunched under the vehicle's tires. Fifty feet south of where she had hid her patrol vehicle, the other car pulled off the gravel, tapped the brakes, and coasted slowly toward the river.

Tru reached for the night-vision goggles and fixed their lenses on the windows of the car. The flash of a quickly tapped brake light glared and snapped off again. She lifted the night goggles up to her eyes.

Tru watched the lone occupant steer with one hand while appearing to struggle with something on the passenger side. The vehicle abruptly halted. The brake lights came on with a final thrust, and the car jarred to a halt under the spreading bare limbs of an elm. The driver flung himself onto the passenger's seat and disappeared. A moment later his head popped back into view as he roughly shifted something against the passenger-side door. Tru believed she saw another pair of flailing arms feebly trying to fend off the aggressions of the driver.

Tru picked up the radio microphone and quickly called in the location, requesting backup.

Unit 756 responded. "Might not be your guy. They dump garbage down there too, detective," the weary tones of a male patrol officer suggested.

"Then we'll arrest him for littering. But I think this guy is wrestling with someone. You need to hurry," Tru snapped at the officer as she tossed the microphone on the car seat and tried to quietly exit the vehicle. With the night-vision goggles securely snapped in place, she noiselessly walked toward the other car.

She hoped she would not find some environmentally-impaired idiot tossing bags of dirty diapers or empty beer cans down the riverbank.

Tru jogged toward a narrow line of trees near the graveled parkway turnaround. As she knelt down she focused on the interior of the car. In the green glow of the goggles, Tru saw the driver violently shake someone with long hair. She watched as the victim's head snapped back and forth in loose, yielding motion. A series of low, cursing barks erupted from the infuriated driver and punctured the stillness of the night.

Tru took the goggles off and jogged as quietly as she could toward the rear of the vehicle. She crouched silently near the bumper on the driver's side and willed her breath to come in easier gulps. The idling hum of the car did not mask the continued sounds of struggle in the front seat. Tru could hear the sounds of a hard, closed fist striking soft flesh, followed instantly by the sounds of explosive gasps of pain. Tru's eyes searched the dark, rolling swell of the park and distant roadway, hoping to see the swiftly moving light of the responding patrol unit. She was not too surprised to find the road dark, signaling that her backup had not yet entered the park.

Her heart was pounding in her chest as she lifted the 9 mm from its holster, raised herself up, and walked carefully toward the driver's open window. She had the element of surprise on her side and intended to use it. Watching the interior, she saw the driver shove his victim against the door. Carefully, Tru reached for the door handle as the quick, flickering glare of a cigarette lighter briefly brightened the inside of the car.

She chose that moment to jerk open the driver's door and shove her 9 mm at the driver.

"Hands up, asshole," Tru commanded.

"What the —" the man choked, dropping his cigarette.

"Police. Now, let me see both of your hands. Slowly," Tru cautioned the man. "You over there, can you get out?" Tru asked the beaten passenger.

"Officer —" the driver stuttered.

"Turn off the engine and get those hands up on the dash. Now! I won't ask again," Tru threatened as she heard the passenger open the door.

"Easy now. I can explain —" the driver persisted.

"Damn right, you'll explain," Tru asserted. She heard the distant whine of the responding patrol car heading her way. Relief swept over her and then vanished as she heard a body falling hard on the ground. She glanced at the open passenger door and wondered how seriously injured the person might be.

"Sent for help, didn't you?" The driver's gritted question drifted toward Tru.

Abruptly, Tru returned her attention to the driver in time to see him grab the shift lever on the car's steering column. As he slammed the car into drive and slapped his foot on the accelerator, Tru lunged at him through the open window.

The car jerked forward, the door frame striking Tru's ribs and back viciously. She lost the grip on her 9 mm.

The driver and Tru fought over the steering wheel as the car lurched forward. In frustration, he pounded at Tru's head and shoulders with his right fist as the car accelerated wildly over the embankment and toward the river.

Tru wrenched at the wheel for safety and tried to pull herself through the window, her feet dangling above the grass.

The vehicle careened down the bank and toward the rock-and-boulder-buttressed waterway. Tru managed to punch the driver once before the vehicle collided with the boulders at the river's edge. The impact slammed Tru into the windshield, stunning her as the vehicle launched itself a few feet into the air. The car made a lazy half roll and dumped Tru into the interior as it dropped toward the swiftly flowing river.

Tru's head hit the roof of the car a second time before the driver's body slammed into her as the flipping car hit the water. The Big Blue poured through the open doors and windows and instantly submerged the car.

A cold strangling darkness engulfed Tru. She gulped water into her lungs. She fought down panic as the fluid blackness of the river choked and gagged her. She kicked wildly and bumped her head against the car's rear window. Reorienting herself, she turned around, crawling and scrabbling through the black water where she hoped she would find an open window. A body blocked her exit. She moved it aside.

Tru swam out the window, reached back inside, grabbed hold of a jacket sleeve, and pulled the man through the window after her. Her feet touched the river's bottom, and the deep oozing mud sucked at her legs. She kicked, pulled, stepped onto the door frame, positioned her legs beneath her, and surged as hard as she could toward the surface.

She held on to the dead weight of the driver and struggled up until her hand found purchase on the upturned undercarriage of the car. The angle of entry into the mud and water of the Big Blue had left the rear wheels sticking up in the air. She held on as the strafing lights of a patrol car flashed over the muddy waters. Tru pulled at the limp driver and managed to get his torso onto the undercarriage and hold him there while emergency vehicles approached. Tru wondered at the numbness enveloping her body. Her head felt suddenly lighter, and something felt like it snatched her up, lifting her far above the confusion near the river.

"Some people are born lucky," Major O'Donoghue remarked, as she eyed Tru North to see if she was paying attention. "That's something of an under-statement with you, however."

Tru opened her eyes to find a nattily-dressed spry woman with gray hair reading a metal flip-chart near the end of the bed. Tru looked around and began to realize she was lying in a hospital room. The idea struck her as funny.

"What time is it?" Tru asked.

"Doesn't matter. Not like you're going anywhere real soon," Major O'Donoghue chided as she placed the medical chart back into the holder on the end of the bed.

Tru tried to focus on the dawn-colored room. "How long have I been here? Where did those flowers come from?"

"The lobby store," the Major said, glancing at the large bouquet that was sitting on the chest of drawers. "This room was absolutely cheerless, and you know how I feel about that. I had one of the orderlies fetch them up first thing after I arrived."

"Make yourself comfortable." Tru tried to sit up but fell back against the pillow at the sudden throbbing of her head. "Why can't I move?" Tru asked as she felt her voice tightening in panic.

"Easy. They've got you in traction, neck brace, and bandage on your head. I imagine the medication they've been pumping into you might have something to do with it as well. You had one hell of a time out there."

"What's wrong with me?" Tru asked.

"If I told you that you had been in an accident, I'm afraid that would be making light of the situation," O'Donoghue said as she approached the hospital bed, trying to keep the concern from her eyes.

"You have a peculiar way about you. So what are you, my nurse or my doctor?" Tru asked as a cascade of glittering lights floated in front of her eyes and distracted her.

"Doctor? Are you trying to be funny, Tru?"

"No," Tru said as a screaming pain near her temples joined the lights in her head. "And . . . and if you're not my doctor . . . I think I would like to see one now," she asserted as the room vanished into sudden darkness.

CB Belpre marched in quickstep down the hospital corridor to the room the receptionist had indicated. She had arrived by chance, and her breathing was quickened as she imagined the terror of Tru's reported injuries.

She had gone to the station house an hour early for duty and overheard one of the emergency medical team drivers talking about an injured female police officer. She would have ignored the conversation and gone on about her business, but the driver mentioned the officer's name.

"Tru North. Can you imagine? Somebody's daddy had a sense of humor." The driver had chuckled at his fellow technicians.

CB had fairly leaped at him, demanding to know everything about the incident. Most important, she wanted to know where Tru had been taken. She leaned over him, and the startled driver told her.

She stood for a moment outside the critical care unit wing, gathering her courage before heading past the nursing station. There were no doors to the rooms in the critical care unit, only light curtains that would not impede the people and equipment should immediate response become necessary.

As she walked into the room, CB was surprised to see an older woman. The woman, her back ramrod straight, was looking out the window near the corner of the room. One shoulder betrayed a weariness of burdens.

CB looked at the curiously small body lying in the hospital bed. Tubes, intravenous needles, and electronic monitors were attached in webbed confusion to the pale-faced Tru. CB's heart leaped in her chest, and she gasped. She sprang toward the bed.

The woman at the window turned to blink at her. "She's resting. They've given her pain medication, and it has knocked her out," the woman said quietly.

A confusion of emotions raced across CB's face as she fought the impulse to pick Tru up and hold her in her arms. "What . . . ? Is she . . . ? How will she . . . ?" CB stuttered at the woman.

"I don't know. I can't get a straight answer from any of them yet." Major O'Donoghue sighed heavily.

"Why won't they tell you anything?"

"It's not like they have to. But I suspect they're not telling much because right now they don't know very much," O'Donoghue said, clinching her teeth.

"I'm sorry. I just heard . . . at the firehouse. I'm . . . I'm a friend," CB said to the worried woman. "You must be Mrs. North, Tru's mother," she said, offering her hand to the woman.

"No, I'm a friend as well. Known the girl for a long time."

CB looked at the pale face on the pillow. "Is there someone else then? Shouldn't we contact her family? I can imagine they'd want to know that she's been injured."

"Being friends, we might be the closest thing she has to family, now that you bring it up," Major O'Donoghue offered.

"Are you trying to tell me that there's no one to be concerned about her or that her family doesn't care for her?" CB asked, feeling heat rise to her face, part in anger at the notion of an uncaring family, part at the idea of Tru looking so gravely ill.

"What? Oh . . ." O'Donoghue said with dawning comprehension. "It would be like Tru not to mention. Not to mention for a long time, anyway. She doesn't have family," O'Donoghue explained. "Tru's an orphan. Always has been. One of those kids you hear about getting shipped around. Life didn't start her off with any real sense of permanency or stability."

"Orphan?"

"Yeah. She mentioned once that she had been rather sickly as a child. That apparently kept people from wanting to take her in. Then, when she got older, most folks wanted infants, not children. Our friend Tru grew up in and ran away from orphanages. She's never had anyone but herself to rely on."

"There's another friend," CB heard herself saying. "Some sort of college professor. Do you know her? A Marki Campbell?" CB inquired, knowing that if the situation were reversed, she would want someone to let her know.

"I've heard some about her from Tru," O'Donoghue responded. "Here," she said, tossing a key she had fetched out of her coat pocket to CB. "There, over there in the bureau drawer. I locked Tru's wallet and leather briefcase they brought in with her. Chances are she might have a phone book or an appointment calendar with an address or phone number."

54

CB stared at the key in her hand. If there was a phone number or address, she would let Marki know about Tru. It was not a call she looked forward to making. It was a connection she had never wanted to make.

# Chapter 5

His prey was becoming more difficult to separate from the herd. The last several months of his ambitious procurements had created a certain terror in even the most self-confident and streetwise prostitutes. He was convinced that he was the cause of their uncharacteristic fidgeting, cautious looks at the cruising johns, and new tendency to stand with their backs against any available solid brick wall. Fear was making them cautious, but not cautious enough. Television and newspaper accounts of his exploits had not been enough to keep them from the street, and he vowed that it would not be enough to keep them from becoming the focus of the emancipation he had in store for them.

It amused him to watch from the comfort of his car. He could see them almost sniffing the air of the strangers who approached them, as if they could sense the advance of danger. It entertained him to think that they believed he would be one of their customers. Amused as he was, though, it galled him that they thought he could be interested in them, in that way. They did not understand; they never would.

The tasks with which he was charged were vital for their redemption and vital for their sanctification.

He knew that neither his prey nor the police were capable of fathoming the world beyond their dense and insipid presumptions. He simply outclassed them when it came to understanding human nature. No one knew the vileness, the repulsiveness, and the need to be cleansed and released the way he did.

Apparatuses of the civic will and pawns in the political and social bickering that passed as commitment to the public welfare, the police were incapable of appreciating the indispensableness of his deeds. They would never know where to look or how. They would never find him.

The media had altered the attention of the police, the police had interfered with the easiness of the pickings he had previously enjoyed. He had to abandon several of his favorite haunts when police increased their patrols. The officers were observant of and curious about even the most minor comings and goings in the old tramping grounds. Having to search for other areas had not been a problem, but it unsettled him that the police had been able to force him to change his conduct. His rising trepidation threatened his preference for casualness, the comfort of the well-researched familiar, and the cozy neighborhood environs.

But the new prowling grounds were going to turn out fine. He had reasoned that it would take a few days, even a week, to feel comfortable in his new surroundings. Composed and poised, he accepted the challenge. He had all the time he needed.

"Idiots," he scoffed under his breath as he watched the black-and-white police cruiser carry two uniformed officers past his parked car and down the next street. They had not directed a single look of attention in his direction. They had been too busy looking for what was easy, the women standing in the loose huddle on the corner, to pay attention to him. Not that it would have mattered.

His late model Chevy was not the sort of vehicle that would raise suspicion. He was patient. It had taken him years to come this far. A careful man, he depended on his intellect to hold his eagerness at bay.

There was nothing to do but hunt, observe, and wait for his prey to offer herself. Once he was able to decide who among the likely candidates would be his favorite, he would make his next move.

He would not bring out the van until he had made his selection, knew the territory, and was ready to act. Then, even the van provided an unpretentious exterior as a standard, run-of-the-mill conversion. It was big enough for a family man, if he had been one. Or it could have hauled tools for work, kids to practice, or campers and their gear on any excursion. But it wasn't that kind of van.

The tools he had hidden inside the tiny cupboards and defunct stereo speakers helped ensure that a captive stayed caught until the body needed disposing of.

It did not make sense to him that the police put everything they thought they knew about him and his deeds in the newspaper. It seemed ludicrous that anyone with fifty cents and a eighth-grade reading ability could find out how the police intended to conduct the investigation, and what they believed they were looking for. Some of it was a game; he understood that. They would plant things in the paper, try to arouse his anger, punish him for his ability to make them look like fools, and make puny attempts to try to provoke him into contacting them.

That would not happen. He had studied them and their techniques. He would not aid them in their attempt to ensnare him.

However, he loved the name the media had given him. The image of the Blue River Stalker conjured up an illustrious enigmatic and miraculous mystery about him. Their reporters' insights had been shrewd, and in appreciation of their perceptiveness, he intended to live up to their flattery. He treasured their devotion to the detail of the cases and the occasional inside information they scattered in the columns of print devoted to him. He wondered what the police thought when the media shared more than what the investigators were intent on spoon-feeding them.

From the comfort of his car, he watched three women huddle under the yellow glare of a streetlight; any one of them would do. They were so interchangeable. Their scant costumes and feigned allure seemed almost comical to him.

The tallest of the trio caught his attention. She strutted around fussing over her shorter and dumpier companions. Through his open window, he could hear her strident voice encouraging and cautioning the women as they sashayed toward slowly cruising cars of men.

The tall one was like a lankly festooned ship sailing between two stout tugs. The walk, the exaggeration of her hips above the clicking high heels, drew his eyes to her hips and undulating pelvis. Despite her best attempt at sensuality, the garish blouse, the too tight skirt, and the incongruously large handbag attested to her shortage of personal style, her limitation of taste, and her beggarly social skills.

"So many sluts, so little time," he mused as he put the car in gear and moved closer to where the woman sailed between the cruising cars and her companions. He wanted to get closer, see their faces better, and develop a more calculated analysis of which might be the sweetest meat.

His quarry had spent several hours soundly unfavored at their pursuit. That situation was beginning to change. He watched as the shortest woman flounced toward an off-duty cab and climbed in. And as he pulled across the street, the second woman climbed into a green Mustang convertible and sped off into the night with her new sexagenarian companion. The tall hooker pursed her lips petulantly at the evening traffic that seemed satisfied to look at her but content to leave her alone.

His mind bent to the calculation of the opportunity that had suddenly presented itself. His thoughts raced. Need and caution battered between reason and implausibility. Impetuousness wasn't his pattern, wasn't his style. He considered letting the opportunity go and allowing his natural caution to keep him safe.

"They won't be expecting this. It's not like the others, and it's perfect," he giggled. "I can have my cake and eat it too," he said as he drove around the block.

His circling caution led him back to the corner where the tall hooker stood. He watched her face and posture, and the carriage of passers-by for the look and tensing that would signal they were undercover cops. He glanced at the vans near the corner bar, trying to detect if they had more in common with product delivery, law enforcement covert operations, or men out for a night on the town.

He slowed his car as he approached the corner where she lounged sluggishly under the glaring flashes of bar lights and streetlights. He pulled the car a few feet past her and guided it easily toward the curb. He did not have to wait long. Her curiosity, comprehension of signals, and instincts were triggered. In the rearview mirror, he watched her saunter toward his car and give him her best got-something-for-you stroll she could muster.

"Come to papa," he whispered as he leaned over and opened the door for her.


He was in a good mood, an excellent mood in fact. Everything was going his way. He turned on the radio to his favorite station, cranked up the volume, and let the music throb in his chest. He smiled and accelerated to the tempo as he headed home. It was late, later than he had intended to stay out, but luck had shined on him tonight. He could catch a few hours of sleep and be ready for work. All was well. Time and purpose had come together as if they had been made for him. He would not have to go hunting for some time. She would be waiting for him, hidden from prying eyes and ready to let his inclinations arise unfettered. That was reason enough for celebration.

He turned off the thoroughfare. The residential streets were quieter than the constant rush of traffic on the Southwest Traffic Way. The giant north-to-south artery dispersed its burden onto minor side streets and householder neighborhoods. He let the rhythms of the music and his mood carry him swiftly to home and a warm bed, as he replayed delights in his mind.

The abrupt glare of flashing red-and-white lights in his rearview mirror startled him. The bursting angry warble of the patrol car's siren caused him to jump and clutch the steering wheel in panic. His startled eyes widened as a supercharged hysteria went whirling through his mind like double-edged razor blades. With his eyes fixed on the patrol car, he did not feel his hands pull the steering wheel to the left. The sudden blaring of a horn from an oncoming vehicle broke him out of his focus, and he jerked back into his lane.

Nerves jangling, he forced himself to breathe, to think, and to respond appropriately as he guided his car to the curb and stopped. The patrol car pulled up behind him, its lights flooding the interior of his vehicle where he waited. He cautiously rolled down his window a few inches and waited for the officer to approach.

Long moments passed as the officer maintained his position in the patrol car. Imagination stretched the seconds and circumstances into a far dark horizon of speculations. The distant scratched and muffled sounds of radio traffic that filtered to him from the patrol car set his nerves on edge. Trying not to attract the attention of the patrol officer, he scanned the interior of the car, checking the seats and floorboards in the off chance he had mislaid or forgotten a telltale item. He couldn't afford any slips and his mind raced to remember the details of the last two hours.

When the second patrol car joined the first, he hung his head on the steering wheel, closed his eyes, and watched his life disintegrate behind his eyelids. Raising his head and turning his eyes to the rearview mirror he felt a sob strangling his throat while beads of perspiration trickled down his chest.

The second officer got out of his patrol car and joined the first officer. They were ganging up on him. They knew something, and he was trapped.

A sudden sharp rapping of a nightstick on his window caused him to bite his tongue in confoundment.

"You been drinking?" the officer asked briskly.

"No, sir," he responded honestly, but he could not help himself from swallowing anxious saliva.

"I'll need to see your license."

"Certainly," he said as he fumbled for the wallet in his pocket. He glanced in the rearview mirror and detected the shadowed bulk of the second police officer poised on the opposite and rear side of his car. He handed the officer his license.

The officer looked at the photograph, raised his flashlight, and held the light briefly in the driver's eyes. "Do you know why I stopped you?" the officer asked.

"No sir," he said, trying to maintain his best and most contrite manner.

"You were doing forty in a twenty-five-mile-per-hour residential zone."

"I'm sorry. I just turned off the boulevard . . . I guess I let my wanting to get home interfere with good sense. I'll be more careful," he promised. The officer did not readily respond or take the light away from his face.

"Stay as you are. Keep your hands on the wheel where I can see them. I'll be back in a few minutes," the officer said as he backed away from the vehicle and toward his patrol unit.

"Shit," he breathed. He knew from experience that the officer was going to write him a ticket. The old "wait right here" had always been a clear signal that he was about to get slapped with a fine. *I don't need another ticket!* he moaned internally and worried about his rising insurance rates. A wild idea crossed his mind and then he glanced into the bright lights of the patrol car and saw again the heavy shadow unwaveringly stationed to the rear of his vehicle. There were two of them, and he did not have any weapons. Not anymore. They were with the woman who waited for him. Not like they would do her any good. He sighed. It would be suicide to chance any desperate or irrational move. He waited for the citation with growing calm and resignation.

A shadow interrupted the glare of the patrol car's lights. He turned to reach for the citation he was sure the officer would want him to sign.

"Get out of the car. Keep your hands where I can see them!" the officer commanded.

"What the —"

The car door was jerked open before he could further protest. "I said, get out of the car!"

"All right, all right . . . give me a second . . ."

His legs moved under him, and he slid out of the car. He stood uncertainly at the open door and then noticed the glint of blue steel in the officer's hand.

"Turn around and put your hands on your head."

"But —"

"Now," the officer breathed harshly.

He complied. "What's this all about officer? I'm not drunk. You can test me." The officer grasped the driver's right hand, pulled it behind his back, and twisted slightly as he placed the cuff around his wrist. It felt like an assault to the driver, and he found himself responding before he could think. As the officer reached up to take his left hand, he twisted away from the officer's grasp. As he attempted to turn, the officer's foot connected with the back of his knee. He dropped to the pavement in a heap.

"That's resisting arrest, asshole," the officer advised curtly.

"I didn't mean it."

"Shut up and hold still. The more you struggle, the more we won't let you. You're making this worse on yourself with every squirm."

"OK," he pleaded and lay still. The arresting officer finished cuffing him, grabbed his arm, and brought him up to his knees.

"Come on, get up now," the officer directed as he lifted the man's arms. The second officer grabbed his right arm, and they hauled him toward a waiting patrol unit and put him in the backseat after searching him.

Once inside the patrol car, the officer radioed for a tow truck and advised he was transporting a prisoner to county jail.

"Wait. Wait. What in the hell did I do? I mean —" He remembered his intention to be controlled. "Isn't this a bit of overkill for speeding? Whatever happened to getting a ticket?"

"Mister, my information tells me that you have a real habit of collecting tickets," the officer said, eyeing him in the rearview mirror.

"Well, OK. I got a heavy foot but that doesn't make it a federal offense," he retorted.

"No, it doesn't. Seems, though, you also don't have much in the way of a memory."

"Memory?"

"Like remembering to pay your fines or show up in court. Ring a bell?"

"Court?"

"Yep. You got three unpaid speeding citations and two failures to appear in Jackson County Court and about two hundred dollars of unpaid parking fines. You may not know it, but not showing up for court is one sure way of pissing a judge off." The officer chuckled as he pulled a U-turn on the street.

The tow truck passed them as it headed for his car. "What's with my car? What are you going to do with it?"

"Just think of it this way. You and your vehicle are going to be the guests of Jackson County for a while, the way I figure it. You in jail and it in impound. It'll be waiting for you when you get out in the spring."

"Can't I bond out? What do you mean *spring*?"

"With two failures to appear and all those unpaid fines in your jacket, you'll most likely be in that long before you get out."

"You have got to be kidding!" His mind raced to remember the name of the attorney he used in settling his mother's estate.

The wheels of the patrol car rolled along the rain-misted street as the prisoner worried that each passing second might bring the police closer to offenses more interesting than his speeding.

# Chapter 6

"Like I tried to tell you a few days ago, some people are born lucky," Major O'Donoghue advised, eyeing Tru North to see if she was paying attention. "Even lucky people can increase the positive aspects of what they were born with if they have the good sense to take advantage of situations. That's a really dependable kind of luck."

Detective Tru North watched the spry, seventy-two-year-old retired police major arrange and water the flowers in Tru's hospital room. Tru looked toward the window and noticed the darkened sky and the glow of streetlights.

"What time is it, anyway?" Tru asked.

Major O'Donoghue glanced at her wristwatch and frowned. "A little bit before six in the morning. Not that you're going anyplace."

*Lucky? If I'm so lucky, how come I've got a cantankerous nursemaid to contend with?* Tru didn't feel very lucky as she lay bound, strung, and wired in the traction device that pulled on her back. The traction was supposed to give her legs some relief from the numbing pain. The combination of painkillers and traction tension seemed to be doing the trick.

"You have an odd sense of humor, Major," Tru said through her tightly clenched teeth. Her head throbbed suddenly as her questionable memory swirled in a fog of shadows, wafting images, and confusion.

For three days nurses, doctors, and friends had worried over her while she drifted in and out of consciousness. She frowned at the major to disguise her own concern about her injuries.

"You think I'm trying to be funny?" Major O'Donoghue clucked her tongue in annoyance at Tru and returned to her bedside chair.

Tru shifted ever so slightly to relieve the numbing sensations in her butt. A barbed, angry pain electrified her right hip. She sucked in her breath sharply. "This doesn't feel very funny," Tru remarked as the pain eased to a tolerable level.

"It shouldn't, and it's not going to for quite a while. The doctor said that you'll likely be here for the better part of the week and that when you go home it will be under care."

"Are you going to tell me why I'm lucky?"

"If you don't know then I'd have to say you'll have all the time you need to think about it," Major O'Donoghue scolded lightly. She picked up the book she'd been reading before Tru had awakened.

Tru grinned in irritation at the top of the major's bowed head. The billow of steel-gray hair made O'Donoghue look like an aged Gibson girl. Tru knew, however, that there wasn't much of the deferential girl about the retired major. O'Donoghue was a legend to be reckoned with in the Kansas City, Missouri, police department. She had come of age and risen through the ranks of the department during a time when women had been relegated to positions as matrons and juvenile officers. She had been an anomaly. Years ahead of her time on the police force, she had become the wheel and grease for other women to enter law enforcement without ever knowing why or how the path had been made a bit smoother.

Tru had met O'Donoghue while taking classes at the University of Missouri at Kansas City. O'Donoghue had been a tough teacher and a principled mentor. They had become friends and continued their association after O'Donoghue retired from the university. Tru had come to understand the difference between the major's apparent exterior and the gentle nature hidden beneath the ready facade. The major rarely and reluctantly acknowledged compassion and sentimentality.

Tru closed her eyes and drifted into the soothing ease of sleep. When she woke up again, the room was filled with the glare of the early morning sun.

"What are you doing here at this hour?" Tru asked uncertainly when she recalled that the Major had been sitting by her bedside since dark.

"It's my shift, if you must know," Major O'Donoghue said, never glancing up from the book she was reading.

"Your shift?"

"That is right. Your other two friends have real jobs. Seeing how they are fairly reasonable girls, it didn't take too much to convince them that being retired meant I could stay with you later while they got some well-deserved sleep. This whole mess gave everybody quite a fright."

"Girls? What girls?"

"You hit your head in that accident, didn't you? I thought so."

"Could be. I don't remember." Tru sighed helplessly.

"My point exactly."

"Major, please . . . " Tru said as irritation began to stir in her voice.

"You've been in and out of it for days. The way that car looked, I'd say you're lucky to be alive. Those two girls think so, too. The doctor has had a hell of a time keeping them out of here while you went through one crisis after another. They fought past him and the administration of this place. Seems they've taken the idea of extended family to new levels. They have been holding vigil over you. Opposite sides of the bed, but here, nonetheless. Only caught them glaring at each other once or twice. You certainly have some fiercely loyal . . . is *friends* the right term?"

"Marki and CB were here together?" Tru asked as the realization sank in.

"Not what you'd call together. Seems as though you never bothered to formally introduce them to each other. You didn't, did you?"

"It didn't seem like a good idea," Tru acknowledged slowly.

"Really . . . ? I can't begin to imagine why." Major O'Donoghue grinned wryly. "Well, they've met now. As it stands, they're one of the reasons I figure you're a very lucky young woman."

"Oh?"

"Somewhat, although, if I've got this figured right, the chances of your young hide getting some comeuppance about your double dalliance are rather good. If you're lucky, your friends might wait for you to fully recover before they take you to task. Doesn't seem to be in either of their natures to kick you while you're down."

"That *is* lucky," Tru responded sarcastically.

"That's part of it, but you know good and well it's not the half of it."

"You're going to tell me the rest, I suppose?"

"No, I'm not. If you're too bullheaded and stubborn to figure it out, well, let's hope you take this opportunity to work through it. If you don't, you're likely to keep building that neat little wall you have going up around you. I'd hate to think you'll keep it until you do yourself some real damage," Major O'Donoghue said quietly.

"That the voice of experience, Major?" Tru shot back.

Major O'Donoghue raised a wary eyebrow at Tru. "Does it matter if it's right?"

"Where's the doctor? How long am I going to be in this contraption, anyway?" Tru complained as a wave of nausea swept over her. "What is this contraption in my arm?"

"That's a pain pump. The trigger button is under your right hand. Seems as though they're expecting your recovery to be a bit painful but don't want it to get out of control."

"How bad am I hurt?"

"I'd rather let the doctor talk to you. I don't want to make any mistakes, encourage you, or frighten you, and my knowledge of medicine could do both. Anyway, if you start hurting too much, that thing will administer a bit of painkiller. You can't overdo it, they've made certain of that. But you're supposed to feel some pain, they said. You don't want to get addicted to that stuff."

"What time is the doctor supposed to be here?" Tru said, anxiously eyeing the structure that she was strapped into.

"I'm sure she'll be along shortly. Do you want me to call the nurse?"

"No. I don't like this. What happened?"

"You don't remember?" Major O'Donoghue asked in growing concern.

"No . . . yes . . . I'm not certain. I can't get hold of it." Tru felt an unaccustomed swirl of panic rising in her mind. She took several long, deep breaths to control her anxiety.

"It's a long story, but we've got some time before your friends or the doctor show up. So, I'll fill you in before your morning really goes to the crapper."

"Marki and CB are coming here this morning?" Tru asked woefully.

"Every day. I told you, they've been taking turns sitting with you. Sometimes they're here together.

They don't appear to want to share their time with you, but they show up just like clockwork at eight."

"Somehow, unconsciousness has its appeal," Tru mumbled.

"I'd say you've been doing enough of that lately, and with your eyes wide open."

"Oh goddess," Tru exclaimed, startled.

"What, what? Are you all right?" Major O'Donoghue asked, alarmed.

"Poupon. Has anyone been taking care of Poupon?"

"Hell." O'Donoghue snorted. "I thought you were in pain, and all you can think about is that devil cat."

"He is not a devil. He's just got a bit of an attitude. You should have seen him before he got fixed."

"I can imagine. But don't worry. He's fat, happy, and as disagreeable as ever. Snarls, spits, and growls at me every time I walk into your place. I got tired of it, so I gave the chore to your lady friends."

"Must be quite a key swap going on," Tru commented in swelling trepidation.

"No swapping to it. I made copies. You weren't in any shape to make decisions, and I wasn't going to play favorites between CB and Marki. Not like you had either," O'Donoghue said, tossing another verbal barb at Tru.

"Great," Tru groaned. The idea of the three most important people in her life having unfettered access to papers, journals, and home gave her no comfort. Although she would trust any one of them with her life, she didn't trust anyone with its details. Her apartment contained things that defined her and revealed her, that she kept hidden from prying eyes.

She did not want anyone running across bits and pieces she had safely dissociated from herself.

"Well," Tru said, clearing her throat. "This could certainly put an uncomfortable new spin on my life." She fumed silently, remembering Marki's prodding to be more personally revealing, to be open, to share with her the *who, what, when, where,* and *why* of her life. She remembered the trained psychologist and moaned inwardly. Marki was a lover and companion. The last thing Tru wanted was for Marki to satisfy her curiosity about "the lost years," as she referred to Tru's life in general and the times before law enforcement in particular.

Then there was CB. Wise and worldly CB, who made her feel genuine passion. Tru trusted that CB would never invade where Tru was reluctant.

"The trials and tribulations make us grow and become stronger," O'Donoghue offered.

"So say you," Tru grumbled in rising anxiety. "Things are not going the way I had planned. This could have waited until I was ready, until I was better prepared."

"Life has its own sense of timing. It's the way of the world." O'Donoghue glanced up at the wide, glass-lined walls.

"And here comes your first visitor."

Tru's startled eyes widened expectantly, imagining Marki and CB advancing in unison and bearing down on her. To her amazement, Lieutenant Haines arrived like a battle cruiser steaming toward her trapped position. He had said he was interested in helping her advance in her career. She wondered if she could trust him. She knew the old-boy system had been bad, but this new boy was more difficult to figure. Tru wondered if his demeanor were real or a bureaucratically decorous camouflage.

Seeing her awake as he entered the door, Lieutenant Haines grinned broadly.

Her commander beamed at her. It was going to be a very long day. Tru smiled wistfully at the lieutenant and punched the button on the intravenous medication pump.

The smile stayed fixed to her lips as she escaped into self-induced sleep.

# Chapter 7

At the Chimney Rock County Jail, the days and nights slipped into a stream of sameness for Valerie Blake. She was given the option of wearing her own clothes on the second day of her stay. She took the option. Blue jeans and T-shirts were far more comfortable, and she no longer felt as though she looked like some ridiculous clown.

Valerie's time was taken up reading books from the library, exercising in the small concrete yard fenced by barbed wire, and writing in her journal.

Hungering for entertainment, she began to take special note of the life and people who populated the lilliputian keep. She discovered that she was surrounded by interesting and diverse people. Jail was better than television, only the actors were real. She learned that some stereotypes have more than a glimmer of reality to them. Broad categories, hints of the authenticity of other lives, and a smidgen of the world of eccentrics began to reveal themselves.

Clean and sober, she found that she enjoyed talking to people and reading. Sobriety provided her with a brighter clarity about herself and her situation than she had enjoyed for years. Tentatively, while using others for a mirror to her emotions, she considered making some real changes in her life. An assortment of personalities unfolded before her. People who had been raised differently added a twist of experiences. They came down on the side of issues according to their preferences and biases from life histories she did not share. But there were similarities that made her smile. The speed of life in a small town gave rise to more than a few questions about the pace and rationale of big-city life. If it had not been for the bars that stood between them, it would have felt a little bit like home.

She studied the sheriff's staff who flowed in and out of the jail. Her first study was jailer/ dispatcher John Dawes. It did not take long for her to be convinced that he was one of the nicest men she had ever met. He didn't seem like a jailer at all. Valerie had met enough to know the difference between Dawes and her previous jailers.

He brought in two-gallon tubs of ice cream, bought with his own money, as late-night snacks for the inmates. John would come to her cell and drop huge, rounded scoops of the stuff into a bowl on the cart he pushed ahead of himself. He would hold the bowl out and tell her there was plenty more if and when she wanted it. Sometimes he would stay a moment or two and talk to her, fill her in on the news of the day, and let her know what the weather was doing outside. More interesting for Valerie was the fact that he actually talked with her as if she was more than an inmate.

Sheriff Clayton Heyenn was more complex and difficult for Valerie to get a fix on. In the first week of her stay, she did not have the opportunity to talk to him more than twice, but she did not feel that his behavior was unusual. He was the sheriff. Tiny town jail or not, he had no real reason to have a conversation with her outside the performance of his duty. For her part, Valerie understood that his functions were to keep the operation of the jail smooth, settle disputes when they arose, and mete out punishment if the occasion demanded it.

Still, Sheriff Heyenn wasn't what Valerie had expected. Not physically. He was small, wore bifocals, and looked like an accountant, thoughtful and formal in his personal presentation. Valerie had been pleased when she managed to make him laugh during their first meeting. He had surprised her by asking if there was anything that he might do to make her stay more comfortable. She had not hesitated. She told him she wanted to wear her own clothes and get rid of the jumpsuits they kept putting her in.

He'd faltered and explained that he wouldn't allow her to wear tank tops or short-short cutoff blue jeans.

Valerie blinked slowly at him in wonder, then confessed that she had never considered wearing such things because she wasn't the Barbie-doll type. She reached down, pulled up the long, oversized sleeve, and showed him a tattoo on the pad of her right thumb. A lambda emblem stood in sharp relief to her pale skin.

He'd been startled at her response and laughed before he could stop himself. "I'm not as backwoods as you might think, young lady. I do know what that means."

"I was just trying to put your mind at rest, sheriff. About the clothes thing."

"Whatever. More particularly, see that you behave yourself," he said, putting a stern look on his face for effect. "You know what I mean?"

"Yes, sir."

"Now and in the future. If we get another woman in here, I don't want any funny business going on. Do I make myself clear?" he asserted.

"Absolutely. I've never forced myself on anyone," Valerie declared.

"No funny stuff period, with or without force, with or without a willing partner," he said as his face shaded toward pink.

"If that's the way you want it, sheriff," she said, barely managing to keep from chuckling.

She got her own clothes the next day.

Heyenn's wife was a very different story from her laconic husband. Eloise Heyenn was jovial, corn fed, and seemingly delighted to be anywhere. She was cook and women prisoner's matron, but providing meals for the prisoners was her priority. Twice a day, Valerie could hear her clattering about in the puny jail kitchen beginning at five in the morning. A few seconds later the hollow tin whine of a local country-and-western radio station would drift down the hard, cinder-block walls toward Valerie's cell. It was her cue; breakfast would be ready within the hour.

Pancakes, eggs, biscuits, sausage gravy, and all the coffee or milk you could drink arrived piping hot every morning. The same thing every day. Valerie had not eaten that much in a long time. Trouble was, it was almost too much. Late lunches of stew, hot bread, steaming vegetables, and coffee caused Valerie to worry about getting fat.

The tiny jail became the most interesting education she had ever had. She remembered her grandfather telling her, "Val girl, life is an education, and there's always tuition. Don't pay for the same class twice." It wasn't the first time she knew him to be right.

Valerie slowly began to realize there was more to people, the world, and the way people lived than the usual confines of the street she had called home for the last ten years. She thought she used to know that, but the street had been so hard that she almost forgot why she ran away from Wyoming.

Here were people with whom she could soberly discuss their view of the world and their accompanying behavior, and not have to worry what they wanted from her. Their views and sophistication were no more extensive and no less genuine than her view.

Two weeks into her stay at the Chimney Rock Jail, Valerie remembered something the social worker at the Jackson County Jail had told her, "Differences and disagreements do not invalidate the realities of either party. Everyone lives a bit differently. None of us have a corner on superiority or stupidity. What we do have is the need to take responsibility for our lives. That goes beyond surviving and gets on with living." As the month passed, she believed she might be beginning to sense what the social worker had been trying to tell her.

During the first month the only thing she knew about the other inmates who shared the little jail with her was the sound of their male voices coming from down the distant hall. The barrier of space suited her.

Then quite suddenly one day, the sounds disappeared. The sudden absence of the low rumbling ruckus made her curious. When John Dawes brought her supper, she decided she had to have a few answers. She hoped he would be obliging.

"Sure is quiet in here," Valerie observed as she scooped her spoon into the steaming bowl of stew. He had brought her coffee and milk to wash down the stew and fresh baked biscuits. The thing missing was a nice big slice of pie. Jail or no, she was serving better time inside than she ever had on the street.

"Kinda nice, if you ask me," Dawes observed as he leaned against the cell door. "About time we got rid of those yahoos. Them and their bellyaching made it about the longest two months I ever worked here."

"What happened to them?"

"Time was up. They were two cousins. Got into a messy ole bar fight here a while back. Broke the place up pretty good, too. Got two months from Judge Warner and a bill for the damage."

"They got let go?"

"Had to. Their time was up. Can't keep 'em simply cause you know they'll be back in a month or two. Those boys never have learned how to behave."

"Boys?"

"Only in their minds." Dawes chuckled at Valerie's surprised look. "Those boys are forty and forty-five years old. Been trying to knock the crap out of each other for better than thirty years. One of them might get it done one day. Be a pity. They're the only friends they got, and they couldn't do without each other. They simply get on a tear and get stupid about it every now and again," Dawes explained.

"Anyone else in jail here?"

"Not a soul. And starting tonight, it's just you and me. If you like I'll go down and get the TV from the men's cell and put it in the hall here for you. Give you something to do, if you want to, that is."

"I'm going to be alone in this place?"

"Not quite. Can't leave prisoners in a building all by themselves. I'll be down in the dispatch office. Someone has to be here to handle traffic from the road deputy. Like I said, that TV might give you a bit of company."

"What if there's a fire or some other natural disaster?" Valerie worried aloud. "I'd be trapped in here, and no one would ever know."

"Don't be silly. Maybe I shouldn't let you watch TV. Seems you may have too much of an imagination already. Really, there's nothing to worry about. There isn't anything that can happen in this jail that I can't handle. 'Sides, if I can't figure what to do, I can always call the road deputy and he'd be here in a jiffy," Dawes assured her. "Since when don't you trust me, anyway?"

"Never hurts to be careful, does it?" Valerie explained.

"Maybe not, but you sure as hell don't do much for my ego. You eat your stew and I'll come pick up the tray later. I hope by then you have a better opinion of my abilities to protect you," Dawes said as he walked out of the cellblock. She thought she could hear him snickering to himself as he entered the dispatch office.

Dawes returned for the tray an hour later. He asked her again about the TV, and she told him that she would like to watch a show or two. While he set up a table to hold the television, he gave her the channel changer and stretched an extension cord to the nearest electrical outlet Valerie wondered at her situation. The idea of being alone in a building with a man, even a jailer as nice as Dawes, had a tendency to unnerve her. Experience laced with barbed, destructive, and unforgiving resonance had taught her all the difficult lessons about trust she wanted in one lifetime.

"Thanks, Dawes," Valerie said. "The idea of being alone in here is unsettling. It'll be nice to have a little noise. Funny, didn't think I'd miss those two fellows chattering all night long."

"Not to worry too much about that," Dawes said as he adjusted the picture on the television set. "We're due for another bunch from Kansas City, I reckon. Sheriff said he was calling them to let them know that there was room at the inn. Gotta make our money where we can, you know."

"More people from the Jackson County Jail?"

"Maybe you'll get a roommate. Maybe some good company, ya think?" Dawes asked.

"Might." Valerie grinned, remembering the warning the sheriff had given her. She figured he wouldn't put another woman in with her and that it was more likely he'd place her in the cell across the hall where they currently stored the mops and mop buckets. It would be a change, though, she thought, remembering how long it had been since she had heard the sound of another woman's friendly voice.

# Chapter 8

The following morning, Valerie awoke to the sound of a key turning in the lock of her cell door. She raised her head off the pillow and squinted into the dim light of the hallway, trying to identify the form on the other side of the bars.

"You 'wake, young lady?" Mrs. Heyenn asked as she pulled the heavy door open.

"I am now," Valerie asserted, trying to calm her racing heart. In the haze of an interrupted dream, she had wondered if some jailer had decided that she was fair game. It was immediately apparent that her imagination had leaped to the wrong conclusion.

"Well, come on then. We got stuff to get done before the day is gone," Mrs. Heyenn said by way of explanation.

Valerie sat up on her bunk and let her feet drop to the floor. She quickly regretted the movement when her bare feet touched the floor's cold hard surface. Sucking in her breath, she snatched at her socks and shoes for protection. "Are you supposed to be back here with me? And what do you mean by 'come on'?"

"I mean just that, come on. Clayton says there's no need for us to treat you like an arch criminal. After all, you've been perfectly well behaved since you got here. His being sheriff has certain advantages, least of which if I tell 'em I need a trustee, I usually get one," Mrs. Heyenn announced proudly, and she placed her hands on her ample hips for emphasis.

"Really? What sort of things do trustees get to do? Or is it *have* to do?" Valerie asked cautiously as she pulled on a pair of jeans. The hair on her arms stood up as they tried to protect her thinness from the frosty December weather that had seeped into the cell. She wondered whether the jail or the sheriff's department had a furnace.

"For one, you get to go shopping. Grocery store mostly, but it's out into the daylight and away from this place for a while," Mrs. Heyenn offered.

"Sounds fine. You're sure it's all right though? I mean, I wouldn't want to be accused of breaking out of here," Valerie said.

"No way. I said there were advantages to being married to the sheriff. And if you stay on your best behavior, there might be more advantages to being a trustee."

"There's not a whole lot of people to cook for. I'm the only one here, aren't I?" Valerie asked as she pulled on her jacket and walked out into the tiny hallway. The television was still sitting where Deputy John Dawes had left it the night before.

"Young lady, one of the things you'll have to get used to around here is the fact that things can change mighty fast. Of course you're right. You are the only prisoner we have. However, that's going to change next week. Clayton contacted the county jail in Kansas City, Missouri, and they were happy to hear we could put a few more folks up for them," Mrs. Heyenn explained. "So what we're doing is getting ready. You're going to help me because Clayton has decided after reading your case file, that, well, you've had a rough time of it. He figures that things like that might happen to anyone," Mrs. Heyenn said as she led Valerie down the hall, through the open doors of the sheriff's office, past the dispatch station, patrol officers' office, and ready room, and out the front doors of the building.

"I was drunk, Mrs. Heyenn, and I was driving a car," Valerie heard herself explaining to the sheriff's wife.

She grinned to herself, thinking how pleased and surprised her AA counselor at the Jackson County Jail would have been at that moment. She wondered if there were extra points available with the sentencing judge for finally being able to admit her wrongdoing. It seemed unlikely.

"Honey," Mrs. Heyenn said, turning around and stopping her headlong flight down the front stairs, "around here there are two types of drinking folks. Those who drink because they like to and those who drink because they *think* they like to. Difference is, those who like it do so for flavor and sociability. While those who think they like it drink because they've got things they would rather not think about or remember. Either way, if you're not real careful you can end up with the same type of problem."

"Sounds like you've known a few of them," Valerie said as she caught up to Mrs. Heyenn.

"Knew a few and still know a few," Mrs. Heyenn said as she turned down the sidewalk. She opened the door of a pewter-and-black Bronco. "What say we go get those groceries and then you and I can figure out what's cooking for supper."

"Deal," Valerie said, climbing in on the passenger's side.

# Chapter 9

"Things could have gone a lot worse," Dr. Laurel Curry admonished her patient.

"Is that your professional opinion?" Tru North asked as she moved slowly around the bed, putting her sparse belongings into the small suitcase someone had delivered two days earlier. Her back ached and she chafed at thesecurely clamped  neck brace she was required to wear. She knew her jeans, shirt, and sweater concealed the bruises she still carried from the encounter at Blue River. Every small move, however, reminded her how much the struggle and rescue had cost her.

"It is and it is also fact, detective," Dr. Curry asserted, shaking her head in perplexity and concern at her patient. "You suffered a number of very serious injuries, and you've not fully recovered from them. Slipping in and out of consciousness for three days running is never a good sign. Additionally, I'm not fully convinced that the trauma to your head won't have some long-term effects."

Dr. Curry knew the detective was irritated at her. She'd had to break her initial promise to the woman and not release her from the hospital. X rays had shown signs of significant head trauma from the beating Tru had taken as the car rolled into the river, and she struggled for her life and the life of the man she had been in the process of arresting. The physical recovery, although slow for the expectations of the patient, would not pose any immediate concerns. However, there were signs that not all was going well. The detective was contending with a form of tenacious and diverse memory loss. Healing would take time, probably the next six to eight months.

"Meaning?" Tru snorted to mask her own apprehension. She had decided against sharing all of her concerns about her actual state of health with the doctor. Hints about issues and potential problems had been steadily accumulating during her week-and-a-half stay in the hospital. Little things, which at first seemed innocuous and irritatingly stubborn, finally were becoming particularly alarming.

"Meaning, I'm giving you only a partial release to go back to work. I do not want you to be driving a car, not while you're on the medication you'll be taking for the next week. I do not want you doing anything more physical than sitting at a computer, and even that for not more than four hours a day for the next two to three weeks. Half days only, and then rest. Is that clear?" Dr. Curry asked forcefully.

"I guess," Tru mumbled. She wanted out of the hospital, away from the bland and colorless food, and back into the clean, nonantiseptic-smelling air.

Tru missed her apartment. She missed having her own space, uninterrupted by the midnight inquiries of nurses and attendants. Having been forced to endure a week and a half of hospital conditions, Tru had concluded that there was no connection between the words *hospital* and *hospitality*. She wanted to see life outside the hospital, sit on her porch in the cold, and know her life was not regulated by the organizational needs of a health-care facility. She wanted to go back to work. Her new supervisor had offered her one of the first opportunities for career development that she had ever had. She did not want it to evaporate. If Lieutenant Haines assigned her to do trick horseback riding, it meant freedom from the hospital.

"Good," Dr. Curry said as she rose to leave the room. She did not believe a word of the promise she had managed to extract from the detective, but she could not insist on interrogating the young woman. From her fifteen years of practice, she recognized stubbornness and denial when she saw it. "Who is picking you up?"

"Ah . . . a friend." Tru faltered. The woman's name slipped through her mind and fell into a dark cavern without leaving a hint or suggestion for her to hang on to. Tru's face blushed heatedly as her heart hammered in trepidation.

"Very well. Will you be staying with them or going directly home?" Dr. Curry asked, noting the reddening on the back of Tru's neck. Her medical mind cringed at the idea that the detective was trying to mask a surge of pain. "Do you feel well enough to travel?"

"I'm fine, doc. Really," Tru lied between her teeth. "Just a twinge in my shoulders. It will pass."

"Well, make sure you call my office and let me know if those twinges get any worse. There is no use in putting up with unnecessary pain, detective. We all know you are built of hardy stuff. There is no reason for you to have to prove it to anyone," she said, hearing herself give the same tired lecture she had given a hundred times to other injured police officers. *What is it about the breed?* she wondered to herself as the door to Tru's hospital room opened.

"There you are!" CB said, as she entered the room. Her conscience was bothering her. During the time Tru had been in the hospital, she'd had more than one conversation with her new friend and rival, Marki Campbell. A curious sense of betrayal and comprehension regarding Tru's behavior had mixed uneasily in her for days. She had not fully decided how to deal with the situation. Her heart and mind knew what she wanted but she would not push Tru. Pushing would only serve to violate Tru's sense of self and CB's sense of integrity.

"Is our patient ready, Doctor?" CB said to the white-coated Laurel Curry.

"She acts like it. Without specific tests, a doctor can know only as much as the patient reveals." Dr.

Curry gave a verbal nudge as she left to let the two women be alone.

"Don't feel like the Lone Ranger, doc," CB said as she stalked over to where Tru was leaning against the bed.

"You're taking me home?"

"Oh . . ." CB chuckled. "I have been trying to do that for months, but I suspect you mean, am I taking you to your apartment? To that, the answer would be yes. Unless you would like to come home with me."

Tru blushed at the implication. The woman was lovely, attractive, and more than a little desirable. Tru may have things going on in her head that confused her, but she had not been rendered senseless. The woman knew her and had behaved as if they were intimates on more than one occasion in the last week. Tru would remember her name, feel an emotion, or titillation, and then everything would slip through the sieve her mind had become.

"Maybe the apartment first. I need to get these wobbly legs on some known, solid territory," Tru stated. This was as close to a confession as her fleeting recollections and pride would allow. "So, where's Marki?" Tru asked innocently.

"I'm sure she's around somewhere," CB stated flatly.

"OK," Tru mumbled sheepishly, wondering what slight she might have committed. "This is everything I've got," she declared. As she hefted the suitcase and looked up anxiously at CB tears welled up in her eyes unexpectedly.

CB saw the tears and looked into Tru's eyes in swelling concern. "Are you sure you are fit to go home?"

"I . . . I don't know where that came from," Tru said. She reached for a Kleenex box on the nightstand next to the hospital bed. "It was . . . it was something about a suitcase . . . and leaving . . . and not knowing where I was going next . . ." Tru said as she wiped her eyes and cleared her throat. "Isn't that the silliest thing?"

"It's going to be all right, Tru," CB responded. She took Tru's arm. "You've had a hard time of it, but everything will work out fine."

"Yeah . . . probably just the medication," Tru said, lifting her chin. "I'll be glad when some of these aches go away and I can get back to normal."

The drive to Tru's apartment was uneventful, except that Tru could not seem to find a comfortable place to sit. Her back ached and refused to rest easily against even the soft cushions of CB's truck.

"Will you come in and stay for a while?" Tru asked CB as they walked across the parking lot of her apartment building.

"Absolutely. I want to make sure you get settled in all right," CB announced.

"Have it your way." Tru smiled.

They walked up the back steps, and CB unlocked the door. Suddenly out of the corner of the living room a dark gray shadow ran yowling in delight at the mystified Tru standing in the doorway.

"How in the hell did that cat get in here?" Tru asked, laughing at her own startled response.

CB smiled at Poupon as he tried to rub at Tru's legs. She looked around the kitchen and living room area where she stood, trying to see the cat Tru was asking about. "What cat?"

"This one, right here," Tru insisted.

"What do you mean?" CB asked. She looked at Tru, down at the cat, and back up into Tru's face. She shuddered in comprehension of Tru's perplexing question.

Then, Tru looked up to see the French doors at the far end of the living room. She pointed to the curtains moving in the slight breeze from the scarcely opened doors. "And there's the reason why. No wonder you're shivering. It's almost winter outside, and it looks like some of the winter is getting in here. Did you forget to close the door when you left?"

"No. That cat at your feet is Poupon. Don't you remember? Or are you playing some kind of silly game here?"

A bolt of consternation spread through Tru when she realized the blunder she had made. The last thing she wanted was to alert anyone to the fact that pieces of her memory carouseled to their own bewildering and dizzying rhythm.

"Not him," Tru said, improvising. "There was another cat near the door. He's gone now."

"Oh," CB said, unconvinced. "Whatever, you need to lie down and get some rest. I'll get the door."

Tru nodded as she bent down to pick up the cat that yowled plaintively at her feet. "Well, Poupon, seems we have a lot to talk about. Tell me," Tru said as she carried the cat to her bedroom, "how's the world been treating you this last week or two? Better than it's treated me, I would guess by your fat little belly."

CB watched Tru enter the bedroom and close the door absentmindedly behind her. She listened for sounds from within the room, and when she was satisfied that Tru was busy unpacking she went to the phone.

"Dr. Curry, please," she told the receptionist. A few moments passed after the receptionist placed her on hold and forced her to listen to the strains of country music being passed over the phone line to her.

"Dr. Curry. Can I help you?"

"We need to talk, doctor. This is CB Belpre, Tru North's friend. The oddest thing happened when I got Tru inside her apartment."

"She's awake and responsive, isn't she?"

"She's awake all right, but I'm not sure how responsive she is. She didn't, doesn't . . ." CB corrected. "She doesn't know her own cat, Poupon. It doesn't make sense. She's had him for years."

"You are sure she did not recognize the animal? She wasn't pretending or making a joke?" queried the doctor. CB's assertions clarified the misgivings and concerns she had felt during her interview with Tru at the hospital.

"Dr. Curry" — CB breathed slowly — "I'm an arson investigator. It's my job to know what people are saying and doing when they talk to me. I did not make mistakes. There's something wrong here. I need to know what it is."

"Are you with her now?"

"She's in the other room. I don't think she can hear me. Is that what you are worried about?"

"Yes and no. What does concern me is whether or not she is going to have someone with her. I don't think we can risk her staying alone."

The door to the bedroom opened, and Tru poked her head through the opening. "Listen, I think I'm going to take a shower. Those sponge baths and steel sinks at the hospital simply didn't do a thing for me. Do you mind?" she asked CB.

"No, go right ahead. I'll be here until you get settled into bed," CB told Tru.

"If that's Marki," Tru began, "tell her I'll try to talk to her later. OK?"

"Sure thing," CB replied as Tru shut the door.

There was a long pause on the other end of the phone. "CB?" Dr. Curry asked.

"I'm here," CB said, her voice tightening in concern and confusion. "What the hell is going on?"

"It's going to be all right. It's not terribly unusual for someone who has had the kind of injuries Ms. North has had. It's like amnesia but it's more complicated. Her head collided in the accident with terrific force against what I can only guess were a number of unyielding objects. Her brain has recovered from the worst of the shock," Dr. Curry explained. "Her X rays indicate that the swelling is gone, but it also revealed that there was some minor interior bleeding. The bleeding and the pressure the brain was under may be part and parcel of the current predicament."

"Is it permanent?"

"No, not permanent but certainly troublesome. There is some reason for concern but no cause for alarm. Most patients recover fully in a matter of a few months or a year at the outside."

"A year?" CB shot at the doctor. "She intends to go back to work next week," CB persisted, trying to keep her voice at the level of a whisper.

"I understand that, and she can go back to work. But she may not be working at peak performance. That is one of the reasons I insisted that she only go back to part-time status and that her work be restricted to desk duty," Dr. Curry advised.

"Does she know that?"

"She's been told, and the release I sent to the homicide unit insists upon it. Rest assured, the police department does not want to give any employee a reason for collecting worker's compensation longer than necessary or a reason for the employee to get early retirement. However, having said that, I might advise you that if you should decide to share your concerns with the police department, the consequences to her career, short or long-term, could be swift and detrimental," Dr. Curry advised. "I've seen it happen before."

"Thank you for that bit of information. You are being very generous with your information," CB said. "I appreciate, it but I find it a little curious."

"You shouldn't. You're one of two people she had listed as significant to her. Her files indicated that both you and a Mary Margaret O'Donoghue were to act for her in the event she would be unable to make decisions for herself."

"She did?" CB exclaimed. "She never mentioned that," she said, wondering when and what had prompted Tru to include her in that way.

"Perhaps she intended to let you know, but she forgot," Dr. Curry said. "Not that unusual from my experience."

"It is, in mine. I'm trying to think how to handle this. Can you tell me to what degree and in what ways, this episodic amnesia will occur?"

"I wish I could. The problem is that it is very dependent on the type of injury and, ultimately, the emotional stability of the injured party."

"Meaning?"

"Meaning that the intensity and duration of these fragmental lapses are dependent on the precise set of injuries. Healing is a matter of her overall physical health. In addition to that, if Detective North is prone to having episodic depression or periodic bouts of anxiety, her long-term prognosis is less positive or clear," Dr. Curry recited. "But, being her friend, you undoubtedly know her well enough to know the likelihood of those being possible."

"I should, shouldn't I?" CB agreed. "And maybe some other people know it, too. You should consider, however, that Tru North has a way of surprising all of us every now and again."

"I would have thought as much," Dr. Curry said in agreement. "For most of us that might prove to be true for ourselves, too. Being a physician has taught me that crisis sometimes has a great revelatory impact."

"Yes. Crisis focuses the mind in ways we might previously have avoided," CB said, wondering at her own feelings.

"Exactly. But remember, while you're trying to help someone get through a crisis, you cannot afford to ignore your own feelings or needs. If you do, you create a disservice to someone you care about."

"That's a nice piece of counseling, doc." CB smiled to herself.

"Wait 'til you see my bill," Dr. Curry cautioned in jest. "Seriously, you may find yourself needing help to cope with Tru's recovery. I hope you have friends as good to you as you obviously are to her."

"As a matter of fact, I think I do. An older one and, reluctantly, perhaps another one as well."

"Good. Use them, and Tru will no doubt come out of this thing in fine shape. And you too."

"Thanks."

"That's fine. Call again if the situation persists or if her memory appears to deteriorate in any fashion."

"Count on it," CB said as she lowered the phone to the cradle.

CB went to Tru's bedroom door, opened it, and looked in. Tru was lying on the bed sound asleep with Poupon purring contentedly at her feet. Tru was partially dressed. Her shirt was off but draped about her shoulders, and her feet were bare.

Slowly, CB entered the room. Tru was curled up on her side clutching at the shirt as though it were a diminutive comforter. CB went to the closet and removed a thick quilt from the top shelf. She walked over to the sleeping Tru, lay down next to her, and covered them both up. As the quilt touched Tru's shoulders, she stirred slightly and rolled into CB's arms.

# Chapter 10

He was so pissed he could hardly see straight. It was everything he could do at the sentencing phase of his court hearing to keep from screaming epithets and profanities at the idiot judge. Three weeks after being arrested and there he was in jail. His rat-faced attorney had cost him a thousand dollars, the fines and court costs had been more than that, and he was at the mercy of a system run by idiots for the next three months. It was an intolerable situation. He would not stand for it, but he did not know how to stop it from happening.

He had explained, pleaded, and wheedled every way he knew how. It had not mattered. The judge was going to make an example of him, and he could do nothing to change the course of events.

Something had gone wrong. His luck had turned against him. It had not seemed to matter to the judge that he had dressed in his best and most expensive suit. It had not mattered to the jury that he had been clean and freshly shaven every day of the three-day trial. The days had dragged by, pressing in on his good nature and his ability to keep his mask from slipping. It had been years since he had felt so helpless and at the mercy of others. He did not like the feeling. It brought back too many memories — hateful, savage, loathsome memories — about his father.

He paced the floor of the tiny cell in Jackson County Jail. Bemused, he invented a game of remembering.

*George Kradus.* He hated the sound of that name and its hollow whisperings inside his skull. The man made him cringe. Weak, useless, insipid little salesman that he had been. At twenty-one he exorcised it from his life by changing his name to one that fit his style and intelligence.

George Kradus, his father, had been a failure at almost everything he touched. *The man.* That's the way he thought of him, but only as a joke. The man who was his father (he couldn't bear the idea that they were flesh of the same flesh) had done nothing with gusto, nothing with fervor. His life had been tepid, prudent, and boring without end. George Kradus had wanted the same nauseatingly boring life for his only son.

He insulated himself from his father. He tricked his father into believing that he was a thoughtful, studious, introspective boy. His father was not one to insist that his son take any other direction. So he was left to his own imagination, his own devices, his own creativity. And he had a lot of creativity.

He remembered, and in remembering his excitement grew.

He was hiding from his mother. He ran to the garage and climbed up into the slat-board loft above the cars. Dirt, spiderwebs, and ancient dust covered everything. It felt wonderful. He imagined he was being pursued by evil, ignorant trolls, deceptively disguised as his parents. He was a prince, captured as a child and now forced to live in humiliation, except in those moments when he could flee their unrelenting control.

He moved a few boxes, trying to clear a bit more space. He moved carefully and quietly, so as not to alert his captors. He bumped up against an odd-shaped object. There in the dim light, something long, hard, and bound with oilcloth rubbed up against his skinny, scraped knees.

He picked it up gingerly. It looked like a thick, dead snake, its hide air dried in some far-off desert and left to turn to ashes in the hot high summers of Missouri.

He picked at the cover. It yielded. His hands explored the length and rubbed across the winding parched string that held the cloth together. Tugging at the string with his skinny little fingers, he only succeeded in giving himself a burning cut across his tender palm. As he licked at the blood oozing from his dirt-smudged hand, he felt a tingling of possibilities rise in his heart.

It was a treasure. Every story he had ever read told him that treasures were never easily won. He would have to work hard, be clever, and outwit the spell placed on the mysterious device.

He groped in the stifling darkness and found a loose ten-penny nail in the boards. Twisting and turning, he freed the nail and used it to turn the binding string until it snapped.

He licked his lips, tasting salt and dust, as he unrolled the magic article in his hands. His eyes widened as it revealed itself. A glint of steel — sharp, evil, and willful — winked at him. It seemed alive, and he almost dropped it when he thought he felt it move in his hands. Instead, he grasped it harder and felt it bite into his tender flesh, anointing him, christening him, and making him one with its power.

In the lowering late evening, in the dusty attic of George Kradus's humble garage, a terrible riddle had wrapped itself around a lonely, shy boy. The boy who had gone into the garage was born again. This time he was not ordinary; this time he was not doomed to the same unrelentingly dreary life his parents had devised for him. George Kradus's ten-year-old son emerged with a vision sparked of fantasy and a short, sharp sword.

Later that week, his mother sympathized with a neighbor over the mysterious loss of her old pet cat. It frightened him initially. He worried for a week that someone might find out the truth or suspect it. But no one ever questioned him. It was the first success he ever tasted.

Through practice and patience, he versed himself in the arts of stealth and concealment and nursed himself into an expanding creativity. As the years advanced, the neighborhood began to be particularly plagued by obscure disappearances of small animals and a number of unexplained fires.

He had never been bored again, that is, until they locked him up for failing to appear in court and for owing three unpaid speeding citations and a fistful of parking fines.

The indignity of his situation appalled him. Then slowly the plan began to emerge. While he was pacing in his cell, he saw the flash of the photograph appear like magic in front of his eyes.

The judge had a daughter.

He almost roared in merriment as he recalled the lithesome beauty's image. Remembering where he was, he hushed himself and abruptly sat down on the cot to focus his memory and begin to weave his fantasy around her.

Her voice would be another voice to add to the chorus that sang in his memories.

# Chapter 11

"This is great. I appreciate you letting me go along with you," Valerie exclaimed cheerfully.

"Make no mistake, dear. As a trustee you are still under the custody of my husband by order of the court and, I guess, the agreement we have with Jackson County Jail. *Trustee* means I can trust the fact that you'll behave yourself, you won't try to escape, and you'll work as hard as we have to," Mrs. Heyenn said earnestly.

"Even if I wanted to escape, I don't know where I am or where I would go," Valerie stated honestly.

"Well, thing is, and you should know, trying to escape, or escaping and getting caught again, would mean a felony charge. Do you know what that would get you?"

"No," Valerie said slowly.

"Two years in the women's prison near St. Louis, Missouri. I hear they have some fine accommodations, but it's not worth the trip," Mrs. Heyenn said pointedly.

"I suppose not. I've got another three months on my sentence, and I'm not so stupid that I would want to tack two years or a felony charge onto it," Valerie said.

"Didn't think you were. Is this your first time to the Ozarks?" Mrs. Heyenn asked.

"Yes it is, but not what you would call by choice. More like popular demand," Valerie said. "Once I got to Kansas City, Missouri, I never seemed to be able to get away."

"Believe it or not, you're in for a real treat. We have some of the prettiest country here anyone could ever imagine. More important, being on the north end of the Lake of the Ozarks has its advantages. We're not as crowded as some other places. Seems like the moneyed tourists and developers haven't discovered us yet."

"Is that a good thing?"

"Most of us old timers seem to think so."

"More tourists could mean more money and more jobs," Valerie interjected.

"It could, but we like it just the way it is. Oh, we do have vacationers. Lots of them. But most have been coming here for so long, they're more like friends and family. It's nothing like it is down in the Branson area. They got more honky-tonk LA folk and Grand Ole Opry wannabes than you can shake a stick at. But up here, we're in the eye of the dragon." Mrs. Heyenn nodded her head contentedly as she made her point.

"Eye of the dragon?" Valerie asked, swiveling her head to look out the windows in question.

"Sure can tell you're not from these parts." Mrs. Heyenn chuckled kindly. "When we get back to the sheriff's department, I'll show you a map. It's the map that tells the tale. You don't even have to squint very much to see the curling body, a hint of wings, and the proud head. I always thought it was interesting to live here." The sheriff's wife beamed as she turned the car down the street.

"I can tell that." Valerie remarked, more to herself than Mrs. Heyenn.

"Call me Eloise. If we are going to be working together, the formality thing has to go."

"You're gonna be my jailer and my friend." Valerie let a hint of sarcasm slip into her voice.

"Only if you want a friend," Eloise said, casting a concerned look in Valerie's direction. "For the time being, let's say that it makes the talking more practical, and I won't have to keep looking around for my husband's mother. In my mind, she's Mrs. Heyenn. That sound all right to you?" Eloise asked as she stopped the car in front of Bryer's Grocery Store.

"I promise to behave, Eloise."

"Good. If you're real good, I'll see what we can do about getting my husband to agree to let me show you some of the area. You'll have to endure maybe a history lesson or two from me. I do love this area."

"Fine by me, Eloise. I'll try to improve on my manners a bit. It's, well, I never expected to be in jail. And I certainly never expected to be in somewhere called the Ozarks and in jail," Valerie reflected aloud.

"No doubt. Let's get those supplies and get back. I've got to do a lot of preparation to get ready for the next batch of folks. Funny. We're a lot busier this time of the year than usual. Must be having a real bumper crop of crime up in Kansas City," Eloise Heyenn remarked as she got out of the car.

Valerie followed her into the grocery store and tried not to feel self-conscious about the looks she received from several customers who were leaving the store. The looks told her that she was not the first trustee Sheriff Heyenn's wife ever made a supply run with. They knew she was a prisoner in tow of the matronly jail cook. Valerie tried to shake off the feeling that she was being closely watched by grocery clerks and customers as she followed Eloise through the store, but it was no good. The eyes staring at her back, watching her every movement brought home the fact that if she did cause trouble, if she merely contemplated leaving the store without Eloise, every man, woman, and child in the town of Chimney Rock would be after her in a wink.

Eloise Heyenn watched Valerie move through the aisles of the store with a caution born of lifelong un-certainty. Eloise felt sorrow for the young woman. Life had not given her an easy road. She wanted to tell

110

Valerie somehow that life could change but that it had to be worked at. Eloise knew from personal experience how comfort and safety could turn on a dime.

She promised herself that if time and circumstance allowed she would take Valerie for drives around the Chimney Rock County edges of the lake. She wanted her to know the beauty and security of a world far away from the maddening life of Kansas City, Missouri. Eloise liked the idea of showing Valerie that lives could be lived differently where people cared about one another and where madmen might be spotted on the street and safely avoided.

Eloise decided she would share the view and history of the Lake of the Ozarks with her. She would tell stories of the early Scotch-Irish immigrants, of the lake area that was once called the Irish Wilderness, and of the rough topography that isolated those early outlanders. And she could tell Valerie how all of that tilted away from the values, lifestyle, and belief systems of the earliest settlers.

At the cash register Eloise turned to Valerie. "You know, I got a little time to spare this morning. What say we go for a bit of a drive and I'll start to bore you with why I love this little spot of heaven?"

"Deal!" Valerie agreed quickly to the unexpected kindness.

Over the following two hours Eloise Heyenn drove down the serpentine roads that brushed the upper shorelines of the Lake of the Ozarks, and along the spine of the dragon. She watched Valerie's eyes widen when she heard that the lake had a thirteen-hundred-mile shoreline, surpassing even that available to the state of California. Eloise hinted at and let her glimpse the grand roll of wooded hills, steep, snow-packed roads, and the chilly hidden spots of fog-frosted lake coves. Tucked as it was in the late fall threat of winter in the Midwest, it was a majestic sight to behold.

The transport from Jackson County Jail did not arrive as the sheriff predicted. Eloise explained to Valerie about the administrative mix-up. She justified her husband's imprecision as misinformation he had been given by the transportation coordinators in the Jackson County court's system. It seemed that all transports had been delayed due to reclassification of inmates. The Jackson County Jail was suffering from overcrowding, but the court-ordered cap on the inmate population had undergone some sort of revision. Because she was a trustee, the sheriff did not hesitate to discuss his own jail operations, issues, and problems in front of Valerie. He and his wife would stand in the kitchen of the jail and deliberate the effect of the delay on the Chimney Rock Jail food budget. Occasionally Sheriff Heyenn would pointedly vent his irritation at having to depend on monies brought from Kansas City, Missouri, inmates to bolster his jail's coffers. Valerie learned more about the operational problems of big-city jail processes than she thought she ever needed or wanted to know.

Emboldened by her status of trust, she approached the sheriff with an idea. She practiced for two days trying to figure out the exact and best way to state her case without offending the man who had granted her small liberties. She waited to talk to him after lunch had been served and cleared away.

"Sheriff?" Valerie asked, knocking lightly on his office door. His was the only private office in the tiny complex. The road-deputies shared a wide-open expanse of a room where their recycled Army surplus desks partnered with each other. The eighteen-by-twenty-foot space was fully lit by fluorescent tubes.

"Yes, Valerie?" Sheriff Heyenn asked without looking up from the newspaper he had spread across his desk.

"Sheriff, I was wondering if I could talk to you about something," she said as she noted that the same peeling yellow-gone-to-mottled-gray paint covered his walls as well as every one of the nine rooms that made up the facility.

"Whatcha got in mind, young lady?" he said as he waved her toward a steel-gray surplus chair. "There something you lack?"

"Not a thing, sir," Valerie said, sitting on the edge of the seat. "But there may be something I might do for you."

"And that might be?" he responded quizzically. He lifted his gaze over the rims of his glasses.

"Not meaning any disrespect or harm, you understand." She hesitated.

"Right, right," he agreed readily and with caution prompted by her slow advance on the subject.

"I know you don't have many staff, and your deputies seem busy enough. What with the jailers having to do double duty as dispatchers and your own wife cooking and everything..."

"Get on with it, girl," he prompted.

"Well, the place is a mess, sir," she finally blurted.

"A mess, you say." He snorted as he leaned back in his chair.

"Yeah, pretty much. Meaning no disrespect . . ."

"You already said that."

"Really, I don't mean to hurt your feelings, but the place is a little dingy. And you all have been really decent to me. And that's why I thought there might be something I could do for you," she said hurriedly.

"For me and my dingy little department?" He prodded and grinned at the nervous inmate.

"Yeah, I mean no, sorta," Valerie stammered in frustration.

"That's a mighty deep hole you're digging for yourself. I'm kinda interested in how you'll get out of it," Sheriff Heyenn remarked as he leaned forward and clasped his hands together over the newspaper he had been reading.

"It's just that I worked my way down to Missouri doing odd jobs. I mean, I can scrape, paint, strip floors, wax, and polish with the best of them. I bet I could even fix some of the torn screens and sticking doors around here. I could get this place looking tip-top if I had the right tools."

Sheriff Heyenn blinked at Valerie. She had taken him by surprise. Everything she said was true. His office and building had suffered from a lack of funds to hire laborers for years. He and his staff had taken the situation as the normal course of belt-tightening by the county commissioners. They had stopped complaining years ago, and he'd stopped arguing with the commissioners long before that.

He could not help but glance around his office and imagine what neat and clean might feel like again. His eyes snapped back to his blue-jeaned female inmate in puzzlement.

"You'd do that. You want to do that?"

"Sure. I mean, I'm already a trustee. I work with your wife . . ."

"I know that, girl . . ."

"Yeah, right. Now, don't get me wrong. I like working with her. She's a very fine lady. It's just . . . well, I'm much better at the day-labor sort of thing than I am at cooking," Valerie offered.

"Eloise mentioned that to me, too," Heyenn responded with a twinkle in his eye, remembering Valerie's biscuits that would have served better as hockey pucks.

"Not like she would have had to tell you, was it?" Valerie laughed at herself.

"Not in the least. So anyway, what do you, as a semiprofessional cleaner-upper, think it would take to get us in shape?" he asked, seriously considering her offer.

"I'd say . . . about ten gallons of paint, maybe fifteen if you include the cells. Wax remover, sand-paper, paint scrapers, brushes, rollers, extensions, drop cloths, a few nails and a hammer, and a big old rotary floor brush. Might be a few things more, but it would be little stuff. I bet you could get everything you don't have for under two hundred dollars. Except for the buffer, that is," Valerie recited as she leaned forward with growing enthusiasm.

"What about working in the kitchen?"

"It's OK, really, but this is more of a workout for me, and I swear I can save you money here instead of wasting it on food none of us can eat," Valerie promised.

"What can I tell my wife when she finds out she doesn't have a kitchen hand anymore?"

Suddenly, the idea of not getting to go on the extended outings with Eloise loomed distressing in front of Valerie's eyes. She had grown used to the drives and the walks with the motherly woman. They gave Valerie a pleasure and peace she had never before experienced. Good hard physical work or a taste of freedom. Valerie hoped she had not undermined her own welfare.

"I could still do both," she sputtered. "It's not like I've got anything else to do. No reason for a lady like your wife to have to haul all that stuff back from the grocer's by herself. Every deputy and jailer here likes her cooking. I do, too. I like, I like . . ." Valerie said, sputtering to a stop.

"I know. She thinks you're a fine person, too. And she's real sorry for your hardships," the sheriff said, finding himself sharing more with the young woman than he had intended to.

"So what do you think? Can we do it?" Valerie blurted, hoping to distract the sheriff from the idea that she wanted to have her cake and eat it too.

"Well," he began, "let me think it over. I want to talk to Eloise. It would not be right for me to steal you for my own interests. Not unless I get her permission first." He snorted. "Now, don't give me that look, young lady. My wife's the cook here. I'm the duly elected sheriff of this county, and I answer to no one but the county commissioners."

"Commissioner Eloise?"

"Truth be known, but it wouldn't do to bring that up during an election year." He winked and invited Valerie into the joke and conspiracy.

"Great. Let me know what you decide. This place could look terrific. I'd make sure of it," Valerie said, rising from the chair. "Thanks for letting me talk to you."

"Not a problem. Now, get back to your cell and let me finish reading my paper in peace."

"You got it," Valerie said, fairly dancing out of the sheriff's office.

"Funny kid," Sheriff Heyenn remarked as he turned back to the editorial section of the paper.


Two days later, while she was lying in her cell, the day dispatcher/jailer Thomas Jordan opened her unlocked door. "Sheriff told me to give this to you and tell you we already own a rotary floor polisher. There was something about the rest of the stuff being bought next week, too. But you can ask him about it later."

Valerie looked at the battered paint scraper and leaped off her bunk to take it from the jailer's hand. "Thanks, deputy. Did he say where he wanted me to start?"

"Look around, Blake." The young man snorted at her like he'd gotten too much dust up his nose. "Can you see any place in here that couldn't do with a new coat of paint?"

"Good point," Valerie said as she watched the nervous young man walk back to the dispatch room across from her open cell block. Valerie figured that the real county commissioner had given permission to the sheriff for her to clean the place up.

For twelve days, Valerie worked as hard as she ever had in the free world and loved every minute of it. The food was great when she contributed less to its preparation, and she went to sleep at night exhausted and one day nearer to freedom.

Two weeks later the Jackson County Jail transportation bus arrived in the late afternoon while Valerie was hauling a large trash container out past the sally port doors. She watched the chained and shackled prisoners marching off the bus and stumbling their way toward a waiting Chimney Rock County deputy. There were three of them, two men and a woman, in the bright orange garb.

It looked to Valerie that things were going to change drastically. After weeks of being the only inmate, except for the occasional drunk brought in by a deputy or city officer of Chimney Rock, Valerie thought that the jail was going to feel crowded. She wondered what changes, if any, would occur with her status as a trustee. She'd had the run of the jail for two weeks. During that time, the sheriff and deputies had grown accustomed to her wandering through the jail and the connected offices. Except for the bars on her room, she had begun to feel that she was at home. She knew each one of the four deputies and dispatcher/jailers. They had let her call them by name, particularly when they asked her to bring them coffee or sandwiches while they wrote up their reports. She had begun to go on errands for them. At first it had been to the other side of the street and the court-house, then it had quickly escalated to most stores in a two-block walking distance for whatever little thing they needed. She had begun to feel useful and valuable for the first time in a long time.

The new inmates and the renewed interest for security they brought with them could change everything. Valerie did not want things to change. Being at the Chimney Rock Jail had become more like an odd vacation from living on the street or in her car and from being afraid of where her life was going and why. The new transfers and the orange jumpsuits reminded her otherwise.

While the transport driver and guard checked their manifest, transferred paperwork, and conferred with the intake officer, Valerie observed the new residents. She wanted to get a feel for the people with whom she would be sharing her little home.

# Chapter 12

Special Agent Douglas watched Tru North through his office window. Since returning to work after the accident, she had performed her duties under the physician's order of keeping half days only. It was a growing source of irritation to the agent. He watched her sit rigid in her chair, maintaining her posture and keeping her back protectively straight. And then there was the two-page case file report and analysis that she had slipped under his door this morning. His hand wrapped around the two-page report and slowly crumpled the pages.

He was tired to death of her less-than-team-committed approach to the investigation. His initial willingness to let her work stakeout had been replaced with anger after she had gotten injured. In his mind, she had diverted much of the team's effort to her own rescue and to the capture of a run-of-the-mill domestic batterer. But the impertinence of the report galled him the most.

He walked to his window and rapped sharply on the glass. She was the only officer in the room and her head snapped up from the materials she had been studying and looked in his direction. He waved quickly to her and walked back to his desk to await the confrontation. He had decided that he did not care whom he offended; he did not want her in his space one moment longer.

"Sit down, detective," Agent Douglas directed.

"What's this about?" Tru asked, reading the thunderstorm spreading across the FBI agent's face.

"It's about this report you felt compelled to give me. Can you explain why you don't know how to or why you refuse to play well with others?" Agent Douglas snarled.

"I'm not sure I understand the question," Tru said slowly, not liking the turn the interview had taken.

"Let me put it another way. Is it because you think you're going to get a promotion that you can, with nothing more than good intentions, try to put together a serial murderer's profile, and cast doubts on the work this unit has previously undertaken?"

"The report was not intended to cast a negative light on any of the previous hard work this unit and its members have conducted," Tru said. "My purpose in presenting the report was to provide an alternative way of viewing the evidence collected. It suggests that all evidence collected thus far be re-examined. Photographs, witness statements, sketches, victimology, everything. I am merely suggesting that rather than depend on loosely constructed inductive logic for a profile, it may be more productive to use a basic investigations approach."

"You've got a chip on your shoulder, detective."

"I don't know what you are talking about. Try to hear where I'm going with this," Tru said, moving back to the chair. She needed to sit down; her back was acting as if it would spasm on her. She had been sitting in front of the computer terminal all morning. It was too much sitting. "Please . . . if we use the profile based on current assumptions . . . we are going to be ignoring some basic investigative processes. We'll be chasing our own tails and getting nowhere. I believe that if we go back, focus on the scenes, lose some assumptions about the victims and the killer, and look at this with fresh eyes, we might stand a chance of catching this guy before we have more fresh bodies to answer for," Tru insisted as she lowered herself gingerly to the chair.

Agent Douglas clenched and unclenched his jaws, grinding his teeth. He glanced up at the clock on the wall and found a way out of the aggravating meeting with the persistent detective.

"Your day is over, North. Doctor's orders. You go home at noon every day. Maybe we can talk more about this later . . . tomorrow or Thursday at the latest. In the meantime, I'll give some thought as to how you might use your time more effectively with us."

"Agent —" Tru began.

"Go home, detective," Agent Douglas interrupted as he stood up from his desk. It was a bald dismissal.

"Sir," Tru North responded as she guardedly rose from the chair.

Agent Douglas watched her return to her desk, gather up the files she had been working on, stuff them into a brimming, soft-side briefcase, and leave the room. He knew he had no legitimate reason to kick her off the unit. Neither his supervisors nor the Kansas City, Missouri, homicide division would buy into the idea that her tendency to annoy him would hold up under scrutiny. He had to find another way of getting her out of his hair. Not fully recovered from her injuries, she was a drain on his patience, and her impertinence at second-guessing proven techniques had been the icing on the cake.

"I'll reassign you," he mused. "Away from the team, out of my sight, and on your own. Give you enough rope to hang yourself, and they'll take you back to save themselves the embarrassment."

When Tru North returned to the squad the following day, she found that she had been assigned to review the case files again and develop a detailed report on her findings. The memorandum from Agent Douglas was terse and precise. She could use all the time she needed, working on her own, and produce a reviewable report developing her own profile of the killer that would be copied and forwarded to her immediate supervisor.

Later in the car, she allowed herself to become furious at the agent's response. It was not his intimidation that angered her; it was being taken out of the loop of information. She had tried to be helpful and was being snubbed for her efforts. It made her even more determined to deal with the situation, to make it work for her, and to pull some kind of victory out of the mess things had become. She reasoned that some things had to start working right again. There were the fires to light on the home front, the flashes in her head that snatched bits and pieces of memory away from her at odd times, and now the threat of a firestorm at work. Drawing on hope and courage, she picked up the cell phone.

She fidgeted with a pencil and let it roll to and fro over a piece of paper, waiting for CB to answer the phone. "Hi there," Tru began when CB answered. "I need some help."

"And you want it from me?" CB asked cautiously.

"Think of me as a work in progress. Very slow progress."

"Is this personal or professional help?"

"Professional mostly, but we might be able to work on the personal too. If you like," Tru offered haltingly.

"I'm not the only person you have to talk to," CB commented.

"No. You're not. But I have to start somewhere. And I have to start where my, where my heart speaks loudest to me," she said. Her words sound lame and witless to her ears.

"I've had a lot of time to think lately," CB replied.

Tru's heart lurched as CB's words rang in her ears. She had known what she was doing to CB and their relationship by continuing with Marki, but she had not been able to stop herself. Tru bit her lower lip to keep from making more of a fool of herself, held her breath, and waited for the sounds of good-bye.

"I want to talk to you, too," CB said softly.

Tru pulled the phone away to keep her gasp of relief from reaching CB's ear. She brought the phone back to her mouth slowly. "I . . . I have missed you. Could we see each other . . . now?"

"I can be ready in a few minutes. Where do you want to meet?"

"I'm outside, in the parking lot of your building," Tru confessed.

"You're kidding."

"Not in the least."

"What if I had said no?"

"I would have driven away."

"Without ever mentioning how close you were?"

"Absolutely."

"Well, that's rather brave, and more than a little foolish."

"Guilty on all counts, particularly the foolish part."

"Whatever will I do with you?" CB said, laughing.

"I was hoping we might talk about that, too."

"We'll see. Give me a few moments to put things in order here, and I'll be right out."

"I'll be right here," Tru promised.

\* \* \* \* \*

At CB's suggestion, they drove to Tru's apartment. The ride in the car had been punctuated by awkward stillness, brief flurries of inconsequential chat, and anxious glances.

"Do you think we are going to get past this situation?" CB asked as they walked into her living room. She moved ahead of Tru, leaving her own unique tantalizing trail of perfume in her wake.

"If we want to . . . we can," Tru conceded. "Where should we start this conversation? I mean, where I should I start? I know I've screwed things up pretty badly. I'm not sure how to begin to say I'm sorry. It's not like I have any excuse or anything . . . shit. I don't know if it's me or this bruise on my head . . . I'm not making any sense," Tru stammered. She'd had more than enough time to think about what she wanted. The events along the riverside and her stay at the hospital had forced her to take stock.

Tru was embarrassed at how cavalier and frivolous she had been with love. She did not know if she could win CB, but at least she wanted to offer a heartfelt apology.

"Do you know what you want?"

"That's a trick question, right?" Tru said, not knowing how or where the conversation was going. She had intended to take charge of the conversation. In that way, she thought she might have the courage to say all the things she wanted to say.

"Only if you don't know the answer," CB responded. She took Tru's hand to lead her to the bedroom.

"Ah..." Tru balked. "We really need to talk." She hesitated. Things were not going the way she had planned. She did not want CB to think that she was unable to be forthright on this side of the bedroom door.

"Of course, but there is no reason we can't be comfortable," CB suggested with a warm smile.

"I'm still bruised from head to toe, and I'm not in any shape to be able to...my back bothers me some. I don't know if I can reciprocate without screaming in pain. Screaming could break the moment, if you know what I mean..." Tru's speech faltered.

CB led Tru inside the bedroom, turned, and carefully took Tru into her arms. They held each other and let the memories of their former embraces flow through them.

Shifting slightly, CB let her hands travel up and inside Tru's suit jacket, slip it off her shoulders, and drop it to the floor. Tru felt herself soften and wondered if the medication was having an effect on her or if it was the simple power of CB's touch.

"You talk. I'll listen," CB suggested as she began to unbutton Tru's blouse.

"Easy for you to say," Tru responded. Her breath caught in her throat at CB's touch.

"I don't think you'll be needing this funny little back brace," CB considered as she unsnapped the stays.

"What if I fall apart?" Tru quipped as she inhaled freely for the first time that day. The brace had helped her posture and ensured that no sudden moves would create aching twinges in her back. But the brace also kept her from breathing easily as surely as it protected her from transitory pain. The brace fell to the floor with a resounding thud.

"I'll be here to put you back together again," CB said as she unlocked Tru's belt buckle, unfastened the pants button, and slid the zipper down.

"Why?" Tru asked, lifting her face to look at CB. There were promises she wanted to make and truths she wanted to speak stuck behind her teeth.

"Because believe it or not, I'm here to stay. I intend to prove it to you often enough and in as many ways as needed to make you believe it, too," CB said, gently kissing the upturned lips. The words that struggled to free themselves in Tru's consenting mouth pressed earnestly into CB's. She wanted to believe, if only for a moment.

The moments became hours.

Tru reached over CB for the pack of cigarettes she had laid next to her lighter on the nightstand. CB grabbed her hand, kissed her fingertips, and laid Tru's hand on her bare breast.

"That's the nicest smoking deterrent anyone has ever used," Tru said as she stroked and cupped CB's soft, warm breast.

"Works, too, doesn't it?"

"Hmm . . ." Tru agreed as she rested her head on CB's other breast.

"Feel like a little more conversation?"

"About?" Tru said dreamily as the glow of their lovemaking wrapped around her like a satiny protective glove.

"Well, why don't you start by telling me why you became a police officer, and then maybe we can progress to other issues — like the Blue River Stalker."

"But if I start like that . . . it could take forever."

"Exactly." CB smiled, pulling the covers snugly around them.

# Chapter 13

Flipper Foxmier heard the scraping scrubbing noise. The sound needled every filling in his mouth. He licked his dried lips and tried to lift his head off the pillow. The shooting pain of a hangover shoved him back onto the bed. The sound grated every fiber of his being; he squeezed his eyelids in anguish.

Weakly he rolled to the edge of the bed. To his great surprise he fell off and onto the floor. The pain in his head screamed. He focused, blinked, and stared perplexedly at the jail-cell bunk.

"Shit," he groaned. "What the hell did I do now?"

He remembered stopping at the Roadway Tavern after work. It was Friday night, payday, and the tavern had been packed with tired, thirsty laborers. Many were his friends and cohorts in the tiny Chimney Rock community. They had two things in common. They worked hard for their money, and a week with a paycheck or cash under the table was a good one. There had not been a scowling face anywhere near the dimly-lit bar. The last thing he remembered was the jalapeño shooters he chased back with beer.

The recurrent scraping of metal on concrete pulled him from the groggy fog of his recollections. Someone was torturing him, and he had to put a stop to it.

"Who the hell is doing that!" he bellowed. He was immediately sorry he raised his voice. The epithet circled his brain in barbwire boots. He heard rumblings in a cell near by. A few moments later as he sat on the floor, leaning against the cold metal of the bunk, he heard footsteps nearing his cell.

"Are you the one screaming at me?" Valerie Blake asked casually.

"I am, if you're the one trying to kill me with that racket." Flipper moaned and looked up at the woman through bleary, bloodshot eyes.

"Not trying to kill anyone . . . I got a job to do, and you missed breakfast," Valerie declared. She had left her cell early in the morning to help Eloise in the jail kitchen. Working was a pleasure compared to sharing her cell with the woman who had come in on the latest transport. She couldn't stand the woman's affected flirtation with the jailers, her air of superiority, and her feigned helplessness.

In the last four days, Valerie had found out more than she ever cared to know about Dawn Haus, bungling arsonist. Dawn had proved to be a nonstop talker with a venomous streak in her. Her boyfriend had jilted the twenty-two-year-old, and she had made him suffer for his slight. Impetuous, lazy, and spiteful, Dawn had waited outside his house, followed him to his new girlfriend's apartment, and poured a full five-gallon can of gasoline inside his immaculately restored 1969 fastback Mustang.

Not satisfied with mere revenge, the petite, golden-haired woman-girl waited outside the apartment complex to make sure her boyfriend got the message she had sent. He did, and he made sure she got sent up for arson of a motor vehicle.

"We've got pork sausage and sauerkraut for lunch," Valerie commented to the suffering Flipper. She watched in growing concern as the man's face paled dangerously. He looked as though he was going to be sick.

"Ahhghh. Don't talk to me about food. Can't you see I'm bleeding through my eyeballs, woman?" Flipper exaggerated.

"Sounds like a personal problem." Valerie laughed. She knew how he felt. She was no stranger to the morning-after blues. She tossed the paint scraper in her hand and missed its twirling form. It clattered to the floor. "And you better keep a soft civil tongue in your mouth. Your bunkies over there aren't the kinda folks to take your complaining in good humor."

"What are you? My mother or some damn fool hell-spawned demon?" Flipper whined.

Valerie laughed out loud at the misery written on the small man's face. She hoped she looked better than he did on a morning after. He was a curious-looking man, to her way of thinking. He was small, shorter, it seemed, than her own five-foot-six and a lot thinner. He looked as if a strong breeze could blow him away and mostly already had. His attitude and tongue were quick with reproach, a trait she had noticed before in many men of small stature.

"I think I'm having a better day than you are. I'll see if I can't get you some coffee later. Might help that head of yours," Valerie said as she sauntered back down the short walkway to return to her task. She had managed to remove all the loose paint in the women's section and cells over the last four days. She wanted to finish the hallway before applying the primer to the walls.

Sheriff Heyenn walked out of his office in time to see Valerie resume work on the wall near the dispatcher's center. He smiled to himself at her indus-triousness. She was a good, hard worker. It made sense to him that an inmate he was holding for Jackson County, Missouri, pulled her weight at his jail. What Valerie offered to do made a lot more sense to him than a number of things his deputies had said over the years. Having an inmate work for her keep rather than giving her three hots and a cot was like getting two things for the price of one. He was sorry he had not thought of it before.

He walked toward the male inmates' cell block to see how a regular, Flipper Foxmier, was doing. As he approached the walk, he could see the two men in the cell across from Flipper's leaning against the bars. The men nodded solemnly at the sheriff.

"Morning men," Sheriff Heyenn said without offering more than firm and courteous response to their gesture.

"Sheriff," the tallest man returned in stoic utterance.

"You fellows minding yourself and getting along?" Sheriff Heyenn inquired.

"Fine, sir. Good food here. Lots better'n up at Jackson," the shorter man replied.

"You're Dave Nessrich, aren't you?"

"That would be me, sheriff," the man said, rising to the full height offered by his small but powerful frame. He squared his shoulders as they had taught him in the correctional boot camp. He knew that the sheriff's eyes would be drawn to the tattoos he had given himself during that earlier incarceration. He was pleased with his strength and cunning. The take-no-prisoners attitude had served him well in boot camp. No one had messed with him. No one had dared.

Sheriff Heyenn saw the jailhouse tattoos crudely scored into the young man's flesh. He grimaced inwardly, knowing that the man had risked all manner of infectious diseases from TB, hepatitis, and worse to engrave the fresh bravado of *wildride* and *Lady Killer* on his arms among the snarling tigers and screaming eagles.

"Remind me . . . what are you in for?" Sheriff Heyenn asked. He had read each transfer's file and was curious to compare the reality with the stories his inmates might conjure up.

"Ah, hell, sheriff . . . a little misunderstanding between the Kansas City traffic unit and me." Dave grinned.

"That all?"

"Well, there might have been a warrant or two about a few things. Then maybe it was that aggravated assault charge they pulled out of their ass," Dave complained.

"Pulled out of their ass?"

"C'mon, sheriff . . . you got the files, don'tcha? Didn't you see where that Weak Willie over on the Paseo had me charged with beating him up when he came out of a bar? It was self-defense. 'Sides, that shit happened so long ago I forgot about it."

"He didn't."

"No shit. So when's lunch?" Dave asked, changing the subject.

"Closer to noon," Sheriff Heyenn responded after checking his watch. It was eleven-thirty. He eyed the taller man who had been listening to his conversation with his cellmate. The man leaned against the bars, arms folded across his chest, and wore a smirk, which hinted of weariness. "You're Jeffery Lahee, then, I take it?"

"Present and accounted for. Tell me, sheriff . . ." Lahee questioned in smooth, artful tones. "Things so busy in this burg that you don't get around to seeing your guests until you round up all the local outlaws?" he asked, nodding toward the cell that held Flipper Foxmier.

Heyenn looked toward Flipper's cell and pressed his lips tightly together at the insolent tone he believed he detected in Lahee's question. He glanced back at Lahee and saw the man raise his eyebrows in comical gesture and grin from ear to ear. The sheriff relaxed. Obviously, Lahee was a dry wit.

"That's my reason for being here," Heyenn said, easing off. "Ole Flipper here gets his first appointment with the judge on Monday. Him being a local boy, I wanted to make sure he hadn't died from hangover. You're not dead are you, Flipper?" Heyenn asked, turning his back on the two out-of-county guests.

"Hell, Clayton, I don't know. I feel awful enough to die and bad enough to be afraid I won't," Flipper moaned. "That girl of yours said she'd bring me some coffee. I'd like to take it intravenously, if you please."

"Iffen you wanted to stay at a hotel, Flipper, you should have thought about that before you broke up the tavern last night." Sheriff Heyenn almost felt like laughing.

"Broke it up? Was I in a fight?"

"With yourself, three bar stools, the bar-back plate-glass mirror, and three or more empty beer bottles."

"Anyone get hurt?"

"Ben Thomas has a nasty cut on his forehead from flying glass, and two of my deputies are worse for wear. I'm afraid no one is in a very forgiving mood, Flipper. I think the judge is going to throw the book at you this time. You've become an expensive drunk. No one wants to go your bail anymore," the sheriff advised.

"Not even my cousin?"

"Deputy jailer John Dawes has all he can take care, of Flipper. He works two jobs, man. That farm of his and here. I imagine it takes every penny he has to hold on to what he's worked for and to take care of those babies he and Harriet are raising," Sheriff Heyenn advised.

"I had money. How much is bail?"

"You had five hundred dollars when my deputies dragged you in last night. You won't get very far with that. Bail's been set at twenty-five hundred dollars what with all the charges. Aggravated assault, destruction of private property, reckless endangerment, assault on a law enforcement officer, and that's for starters."

"Did I hit a deputy?"

"No, but you resisted arrest, and somewhere in the free-for-all Jeremy got his new shirt ripped." Heyenn grinned.

"You gotta be kidding! You going to stand there and tell me I get charged with assault because some deputy got his shirt tore? Jesus, man! Where's your sense of justice?" Flipper whined as he dropped his head into his hands.

"I imagine you'll find out about that on Monday. But if I were you, I'd make some calls this weekend and arrange for whatever you need to be taken care of outside. I have a suspicion you'll be our guest for some time to come."

"You don't whine and bellyache all the time, do you, Flipper?" Jeffery Lahee asked in annoyance.

"Shut up!" Flipper retorted.

"All of you settle down. We've a long road to travel together. Might as well get used to each other's company now," Sheriff Heyenn said. He turned on his heel and walked back toward his office.

"Morning, sheriff," Valerie said to him as he hurried past.

"Valerie . . . fine job," he commented as he glanced at her work.

"Thanks," Valerie responded. The sheriff walked past her in apparent deep thought. She wondered how many years he had been sheriff. The look on his face communicated *far too long*.

Sheriff Heyenn sat down at his desk and glanced up at the dingy color of the walls in his office. Slowly an idea came to him. "Busy hands are happy hands," he mused.

# Chapter 14

Sheriff Clayton Heyenn pulled his patrol car into the sally port of his detention center. As he got out of the vehicle, he pulled the trunk hatch switch and watched the automatic lid snap open. He waved over inmates Dave Nessrich and Jeffery Lahee. A road deputy stood by, watching them take out the brushes, rollers, drop cloths, and miscellaneous paint supplies from the sheriff's trunk.

"When they finish in here, get the others and have them meet me in the staff room."

"You bet, sheriff," the deputy responded as he watched the inmates stack the materials and supplies against the far north wall of the sally port.

"Hustle up, guys. The sheriff isn't going to wait all day."

"This doesn't look good," Dave Nessrich whispered to Jeffery as he heaved the last five-gallon can of paint into the corner of the room.

"Yeah, looks like they got some plans about what they want done with those walls that woman's been scraping off this week," Jeffery responded gloomily. "I hate hard labor."

"You two! Stop the jawing and get back in here," the deputy commanded.

The two men jogged back toward the jail door and hurried up the steps and into the building. They made their way along the brief hall until they got to the patrol officers' staffing room. The other inmates, Flipper, Valerie, and Dawn, were by that time present. The men took their places in two vacant chairs the sheriff waved them toward.

The deputy followed them into the room.

"I've got some good news and some bad news," Sheriff Heyenn began. "Which would you folks like first?"

"Give us the bad," Flipper shouted. He was the sort of man who would eat his spinach first with the promise of cake after.

"The bad news is, it won't cost me a dime except for supplies. Any of you care to make any guesses about the good news?"

Somber faces met his gaze.

"OK, then, I'll simply say that because this place needs it, the good news is you all are going to paint,

140

scrub, polish, wax, and buff this place back to a shine."

"The hell you say . . ." Flipper moaned out loud.

"Deputy, take that man to the strip-down cell and place a discipline report about his lack of manners. I don't want him to see the exercise yard for three days," Sheriff Heyenn directed.

The deputy walked over, grabbed Flipper by the arm, and waited for the man to get to his feet.

"Sheriff, I shot my mouth off. I'm sorry," Flipper said as the deputy led him out of the room. He knew the strip-down cell had no bunk, blankets, or windows. The walls were padded, as was the floor. You could bang your head all day and not get more than dizzy. He would rather have painted the whole Sears building in Detroit.

"I bet you are," Heyenn retorted at the departing inmate. "You'll serve as a fine example of how not to get along, too. Works like this," he said, turning his attention back to his suddenly very attentive audience. "You can go along to get along, or you can try to have it your own way. What I'm asking for is your honest and best efforts in helping me put my house here back in order. You get to be out of your cells, to work and contribute in a positive way in your lives, to do a public service. And you may have other privileges as well. If any of you think I can't have you do this, then I suggest you check the Inmate Handbook you got when you arrived or call your attorney. The plain fact of the matter is, I can have you do anything as long as it's not dangerous, cruel, or unusual. And there ain't nothin' about cleaning and painting that fits any of those words," Heyenn said. He grinned at his hardworking inmate Valerie Blake. She had given him the idea, and now he wanted to see it come to fulfillment.

Valerie was surprised at the sheriff's demeanor. He suddenly sounded and acted like a man who was used to getting his way. She had never thought of him in that light. She had been getting very used to the sheriff and his wife treating her more like a favorite hired hand than inmate. She wondered how the other inmates would react to their new work assignments.

"Hell, sheriff, I'm with you. I'd paint the exercise yard, too, for a little time to work outside," Dave Nessrich eagerly responded.

"Suck-up," Jeffery Lahee accused in a whisper.

"Bullshit. How much fun have you had sitting on your ass for the last two weeks? Seems to me you've been bitchin' as loud as the rest of us," Nessrich responded.

"What would those other privileges be, Sheriff?" Dawn Haus asked.

"Now, there's a lady who knows how to ask the right questions," Sheriff Heyenn prompted, directing the men's attention to the only other female inmate in the room.

"I'll bite. What else is in it for us?"

"If you are working and you smoke, you'll be able to smoke outside when you take breaks. That's a bit more than once a day for half hours as it is now. Extra canteen rations of soda pop, popcorn, fruit, and chew. Lastly, you can wear your civilian clothes as long as you wear your INMATE jacket over it. Other than that, the choice of working or sitting on your butts for the remainder of your sentences is up to you. How do you want to have it go?"

The next day the Chimney Rock Jail was about to get a facelift.

As it turned out, the inmates and the sheriff discovered that there were a few more wrinkles to the new job assignments. The road-patrol deputies were not pleased having inmates wandering around the halls while they were trying to interview witnesses or victims to crimes and generally conduct their normal duties. The sheriff relented and changed the inmates' work hours from daytime to late afternoons and evenings. That created a great deal of grumbling among the inmates. But then slowly, as they adjusted the schedule and eased into the freedom to tackle their tasks in any reasonable manner, the complaining stopped.

From the late afternoon until the wee hours of the morning, the inmates of the Chimney Rock Jail were freed from their cells for their work details. The offices were opened, along with kitchen, pantry, dispatch office, and hallways to make ready for the painting and scrubbing assigned. They worked Monday through Friday and had the weekends off to watch video movies, to phone families, to rest, and to exercise in the yard. But few took advantage of the outdoor yard as winter settled into the Ozarks. The swirling snow, patches of ice, and cold concrete benches made the cinder-block-walled and razor-wired exercise yard even less inviting than its designers could have fathomed.

Visitors never arrived for anyone other than Flipper. His being a local and longtime resident of the community meant that he was able to spend some parts of his weekends talking to friends and relatives.

The distance between Chimney Rock and Kansas City precluded other visits.

On the weekends, Valerie never made any bones about the fact that no visitors would be seeing her. Even if her family knew where she was, she would not have let them visit her. She left nothing when she drove out of Wyoming, and she certainly wanted nothing from there following her, ever.

For her part, Dawn Haus mentioned that she was not concerned about not having any visitors. The only person she wanted to see became an unlikely candidate the day she torched his car. Her parents were divorced and her mother had not bothered leaving a forwarding address. Dawn pretended bravery and bravado, but Valerie was able to see all the cracks in the young woman's frail armor.

The things Valerie did enjoy about the weekends were the ice cream. Like clockwork every Saturday night, jailer/dispatcher John Dawes would bring in three gallons of ice cream, a twelve-pack of soda pop, and barbecued shredded beef sandwiches from the local deli. For all his seeming gruffness, once the sheriff observed how hard and well his inmate cleanup crew worked, he was determined to keep them happy and hustling for him.

During the second week of their volunteer work, Dawn increased her active flirting with suggestive whispers to Flipper, Dave, and Jeffery. The distance away from the jailer/dispatcher and the open offices of the sheriff's department created ample opportunity for Dawn to fulfill her promises. She teased and toyed with them. It was her new indoor sport.

Valerie watched the unfolding of antagonisms and aggressive scheming among the men. She wondered if

Dawn understood how dangerous her actions were or how lethal the men might become.

Valerie found it appalling that every inmate in the jail was treated as a trustee. At night while jailer/dispatcher Dawes sat by the communications system, inmates were allowed to freely wander the halls. They carried ladders, paint cans, cleaning supplies, brushes, and curiosity.

On one occasion and with little ceremony, Flipper discovered that the evidence locker, a recycled broom closet, was routinely left unlocked. He surmised that the large, locked metal gun cabinet adjacent to the far wall was the real evidence locker but did not bother mentioning anything to his cousin jailer. Brooms, buckets, stained rags, and half-used bottles of cleaning fluids were scattered on the floor. He propped open the door, pitched the ruined cleaning supplies in a large trash container, and began scrubbing down the walls. He swept and dusted the nearly bare metal shelving stacked along the wall.

Jailer Dawes saw Flipper an hour later, hurrying in the direction of his cell. He looked intent in his quick march and a little distracted.

"Whatcha up to, Flipper?"

Flipper wheeled around and shot his cousin a curiously startled glance. He turned back toward the direction he had been traveling and shrugged his shoulders. "Nothing much, John. Just in a hurry to take a piss. You want something? Or can it wait 'til I get back?"

The crackling sound of a patrol unit's radio hissed over the dispatch center's speaker. "I can wait," John said, turning away to go back to the radio. "I want to talk to you before you go to bed."

"Sure thing, John."

In his cell, Flipper placed the prize under the mattress of his bed. His heart was pounding and his hands trembled as he reached up to wipe the sweat from his face. He couldn't remember why he thought he had to have it, but it was his now. He felt safer, more in control; he was more certain and much more powerful than the other two rivals for the affection he sought from Dawn.

Dave and Jeffery continued to contend for leadership position as the straw boss. They rankled over it at every opportunity. Their disagreements continued until late one evening when they pretended to go out into the frigid night air for a smoke break. It was then that Jeffery and Dave tried to work out a mutually agreeable solution.

"Look," Jeffery said, hugging himself in an effort to keep warm. "We either get along on this or that sheriff will get wind of just how much freedom he's given us. That could ruin everything."

"Sounds like a damned lame excuse to get your own way, Lahee," Dave Nessrich said, puffing his chest out for effect.

Jeffery did not like the blustering fellow and did not find it difficult to believe that the man had attacked another with a baseball bat. It seemed obvious that in thirty-two years of living Dave had learned little about getting along with people, biding his time, or thinking about alternatives. He seemed singularly focused. Jeffery was convinced that he had managed to learn twice as much in twenty-nine years.

"Do you have a difficult time thinking well, Dave?"

Dave Nessrich's eyes narrowed and sparkled malevolently at the insult. "You know, Jeff," he said, dropping his voice an octave, "There's an awful lot about me you don't know. Trust me. It's better you don't find out firsthand."

"How about we try to have our cake here and eat it too?"

"There's only one little cupcake I want to eat, and I think she feels the same way," Dave said, cutting to the chase.

"Well, why don't we let Dawn make that decision for herself. Girl's got a mind of her own, from what I can tell," Jeffery remarked. "I can live with that, but can you?"

"Not a problem, 'cause I know how this is going to turn out," Dave asserted confidently. " 'Sides, I'm not a sore winner. You can have that other one. She might be a fair piece if she fixed herself up a little better."

"Whatever. What do you think we ought to do about these work details? I mean, if I have to put up with that Flipper crying and moaning in my vicinity much longer, I'll strangle him on his own tongue."

"I say for the time being we convince him that he wants to work with the other woman. Then you and me could have a little more time with Dawn. She's obviously in heat."

"Deal," Jeffery said, holding his hand out in agreement with the other man.

"Let the best man win." Dave grinned mischievously to his new partner.


The following Saturday they found the thirty-six cans of beer and half a bottle of bourbon sitting under the desk of one of the road deputies. Dave had been vacuuming the worn carpet in the deputies' office area. He had intended to talk to Valerie and Flipper about starting to paint the ceiling in the room next Monday.

When he moved the chair in front of the desk to push the vacuum head under the desk, he could not believe his eyes. Or his luck. Then he was saddened. There was no way he could get all the beer to his cell without alerting jailer Dawes. He knew what he had to do. It was time for compromise. And if ever there was a time for sharing, it was now.

Carefully, so as not to raise the suspicions of jailer John Dawes, Dave and Jeffery sent the other three inmates into the room for their share of the beer. Each time one returned, their cache was counted. Dawn showed them her beer and a knife she found in one of the desk drawers.

"What the hell you going to do with that, little girl?" Flipper asked, his eyes widening in alarm.

"Cut you, fool, if you don't keep your voice down," Dawn said threateningly and waved the knife in his direction for emphasis. The cheap six-inch imitation Buck knife imitation glinted.

"You might be sorry if you try," Flipper said, remembering the prize he had hidden under his cell mattress.

"Wanna try and make me sorry?" Dawn heatedly replied, raising her voice for emphasis.

"Shut up, both of you," Jeffery hissed between clenched teeth. "And give me that thing before you cut yourself," he said as he snatched the knife away from Dawn.

"Hey!"

"I said shut the fuck up, bitch. Now get back to your cell and drink a bit of that beer and see if you can't settle down," he ordered.

"That ain't no way . . ." Dave began.

"Any way I can," Jeffery responded, cutting him off. "Go ahead, Valerie, go on, it's your turn."

"I don't care for any. You can have my share," she said, backing away from the ominous confrontation between the two men.

"You go get your share. Anyone who doesn't is a potential problem. You don't want us to think you'd snitch us out to the jailer, do you?"

"It's not like that . . . I quit drinking. It messes me up," Valerie emphasized. The last thing in the world she wanted to do was to get drunk with a bunch of shady fellow inmates.

"Look, you either go and get that beer or you might find yourself really messed up," Dave chimed in, supporting Jeffery's contention.

Valerie started to open her mouth in protest. Her mind was caught between the threat and the idea of cold beer. Her mouth felt dry in anticipation. She did not want to drink but could no longer remember why it had seemed like such a bad idea.

She began to give herself excuses. Although she could think of several reasons why she did not want to drink, she did not want any trouble from the inmates, and she certainly didn't want them to think she had a yellow streak. If they got away with filching the alcohol, there would still be the months she would have to spend with them. They would be a constant threat to her safety if they suspected her of any collaboration with the sheriff's officers.

Valerie walked down the hall to the desk where the remaining beer cans waited for her. Her mind told her how stupid her actions and those of her fellow inmates were. There was no chance they could get away with stealing and drinking the beer. She figured that sooner or later, like Monday morning, the deputy would come looking for his evidence.

Everything was going to hell and she did not know how to stop it. She figured she would get busted with the rest of them, her privileges as a trustee canceled. She would probably get hauled back to court. If that happened, the judge who had threatened her with prison would be waiting for her.

She reached under the desk and pulled out the five cans the other inmates had left to her. She popped the top on the first one, tipped it back, opened her throat, and let the whole twelve ounces slide down her throat. It was an old trick she had learned long ago, and she wanted to quiet the nagging voices in her head as quickly as possible before she had to rejoin her compatriots. She picked up the remaining four cans and walked back down the hall toward the cell block and her new drinking buddies. She resigned herself to the fact that if any of them went down, they would all go down together.

Jailer John Dawes was fatigued and grateful. A full day of farming chores — including milking the cows in the morning and late afternoon, hauling hay for a neighbor, and rough finishing the calf shed to protect last summer's newborn from the coming January snows — had exhausted him. It would feel like a vacation to sit in front of the dispatch console and wait for the emergency phones to ring into the sheriff's office. He was additionally grateful that the inmates sounded hard at work. He could hear the floor buffer droning in the women's cell block as he made his way to the dispatch office He noticed that several had been industriously engaged in painting the hallway walls and ceilings.

He picked up the envelope left by the day jailer/ dispatcher and opened it. The note stated that no road deputy would be on duty in Chimney Rock County that evening but that Deputy Paul Seralls would respond to all emergency call-outs. John Dawes was relieved. There would be few radio calls and no dispatch center traffic as long as no one needed a deputy. He would be able to rest a bit and maybe even feel refreshed enough to begin another long day on the farm in the morning.

He turned on the AM/FM radio and let the music wash over him. It was pleasant. The melodies coated the sounds of floor buffing in the cell block. He checked the volume level of the emergency radio and notched it a few levels higher. He did not want to miss a call if one came. Satisfied, John leaned back in the high-backed desk chair and settled in for his evening watch at the jail. He considered filing some of the case reports, then decided that they could wait. In a few minutes he drifted off to sleep and never noticed when the rumblings of the buffer shut off.

# Chapter 15

"Are you sure this is wise?" Tru asked as CB brought her a cup of hot tea and set the saucer and cup on the wire table next to where Tru's arm rested on the tub rim.

The hot tub bubbled furiously in the cold December air, and the rising steam obscured Tru's vision. Her initial venture outside the patio doors and the necessary naked dash had gone against her body-shy grain. She had managed to convince herself that the high wood fence surrounding the half-gazebo shelter around the tub on the tenth-floor balcony shielded them from potential prying eyes. Sitting in the frosty air, Tru was additionally happy with the shelter's protection from sudden, sneaky blasts of cold air. It still made her feel uncomfortable.

"It's perfectly fine. I bought it last month when I was feeling a little tense. And it's good for your back. I want you fit for anything . . . even work." CB grinned as she climbed into the tub.

"Yes, ma'am," Tru promised. She had spent the last three days with CB, going home only to fetch more clothes. Not that CB would let her keep them on very long after she came home from the fire department.

It had been a thoroughly wonderful time. Tru had the peace and quiet of CB's luxury apartment to work in all day long. Then CB would come home, help prepare dinner, and there would conversation and sharing into the night.

The days and nights of conversation, difficult at first, became easier and easier for both of them. It was like a gift that Tru had never imagined as being possible outside of the movies. Tru's real desires were becoming clearer for the first time in her life. She was finally able to sense what she had been letting herself miss. Tru had heard the saying that time healed all wounds. But it had not been until this week with CB and her lavish patience that Tru had begun to understand that healing would only happen if someone could find where the scars were hiding.

"You have everything you need?"

"At this very moment, I can't imagine anything I lack."

"Your papers and stuff, silly."

"Oh, yeah ... here on the table." Tru chuckled. "I don't know. This feels way too good to ruin the mood with talk of murder." Tru leaned back against the edge of the tub, sank into the heat, and let the water fill her senses.

"Come on, Tru," CB chided. "You don't think Agent Douglas is going to forget about the assignment he gave you, do you?"

"He might. It's not like I'm one of his favorites."

"Fine. But, you can't make me believe your Lieutenant Haines is going to let you off so easily," CB persisted.

"All right ... all right," Tru acquiesced. She resurfaced, reached for a towel, and dried her arms and hands before reaching for the papers stacked next to her. "Kinda pushy, aren't you? And please don't tell me this is how it's going to be."

"OK. I won't tell you," CB bantered. She knew Tru was a bundle of unfettered passion camouflaged behind a facade of bravado. It was her protective coloration, and she wore it well. With Tru it would always have to be one step at a time, find the firm footing, and hold on.

"I'm going to pretend that was a joke and not a veiled threat," Tru said, flipping through her notes as she cast a rueful eye toward CB.

"Whatever makes you comfortable, dear."

"So here's my confusion," Tru said, ignoring CB's remark. "And with your education and experience dealing with bad guys too, I figure you're my best resource to help me figure this out." Tru held up her notepad and cleared her throat.

"I'm all ears," CB said, sipping her tea.

"I've been looking at these crime-scene photos, autopsy reports, and victim-risk assessments until I think I'll go blind. To top it off, I've gone back through my training notes I had when I worked in the pathology department and Saferstein's forensic books. I swear, CB, with every fiber in me, Agent Douglas and his crew are running down the wrong road," Tru announced with conviction.

"All right. What do you think you see that they don't?"

"The first problem I have is the way they treat the dump sites."

"Dump sites?" CB frowned.

"The places where the bodies are dumped — and the assumptions they are making. Of the six women found, two after the formation of the special unit and Agent Douglas, there are fewer than twenty photos per site. No searches are noted or made in the areas surrounding the places where the bodies have been found. I swear they simply run out to the site and hold a press conference. It makes me crazy," Tru emphasized.

"That is not much more than what you've seen with some of the detectives in your own unit, is it?" CB asked. She recalled other times when investigator carelessness, misconduct, or misapplication of principles and practice had left Tru bristling.

"No. But few of those become the sort of media circus this has. Evidence has been lost in these instances because, quite frankly, no one looked for it. Then there are the autopsy reports. You would think that if they were going to try to construct a profile of the killer they'd use the tools they have. Anyway, I think this guy is just getting started. In each instance we have the use of restraints. It's like I told Douglas: if the serialization of the victims has been invalid because we do not have the right order of victims, then this guy is getting better and more organized. Not worse." Tru sipped her quickly cooling tea.

"You're telling me there's a learning curve in serial homicide?" CB said arching her eyebrows.

"Why not? There is in everything else we master, isn't there?"

"Yes," CB said slowly. "I don't believe I'm very comfortable thinking about this as a training process."

"Nor am I, but it makes sense to me. We could have victims out there we don't know about. His early blunders, the ones who got away, the ones he killed unintentionally or too quickly. Any that he didn't feel a need to brag about, and that's what I think the body dumping is about. It's a matter of bragging rights, and he likes to shove our faces in it. It's an ego trip for him." Tru's eyes became intense.

CB felt as though she could almost see the man Tru conjured with her words.

"I hear what you're saying, but why, if some of the early ones got away, hasn't that been reported?" CB asked as she tried to maneuver her mind closer to Tru's thinking processes.

"Prostitutes. If they have all been prostitutes, they would have counted themselves lucky to get away. They would have been bruised, battered, and bleeding but alive nonetheless. I can't think of too many prostitutes who would be willing to go to the police and reveal that one of their johns got his jollies without paying for the pleasure."

"You mean they would have been afraid to confess to a misdemeanor and risk getting arrested if they reported that someone committed a felony?" The desperation of their lives saddened CB.

"Put yourself in their position. If that was your life, would you be convinced that the police would look for John Q Straight or that they would lock you up for your unsolicited confession?"

"When you put it that way . . . but he's simply dumping the bodies. Doesn't that indicate that he is what Douglas claims . . . disorganized?"

"Not exactly. Calling it a *dump* is a bit confusing, and the term *disorganized* compounds the problem. The bodies were dumped, but they were all hidden from immediate view. Every last one of them was concealed in some fashion. Bushes, shrubs, floating along in the river. Some poor citizen out for a morning stroll, looking for a place to neck with his or her honey, or fishing along the bank found the bodies. The bodies were dumped because the killer was finished with them. He had done everything to them he could think of; he had exhausted the sport, and his victim. They didn't die where they were found. They were brought there. He has some cozy safe location where he takes them. And in that comfy little place, he's got all the tools, restraints, toys, and time he needs. See, here's what I mean . . ." Tru said, pulling an eight-by-ten black-and-white photo from the stack.

"Not a pretty picture," CB responded in alarm.

"Oh. Sorry. I get a bit wrapped up in this and forget what I'm doing or saying," Tru apologized as she flipped the photo over and laid it back on the stack. "What the photo shows is a lot of ligature marks, the use of restraints, and a large number of slashes on the victim's breasts before she died. There're some postmortem injuries, too. I won't go into that. What is important is that when this guy dumped the body, there were no ropes, leather, duct tape, or any other restraint mechanism found with the body. No weapon, no clear evidentiary ties. And almost all of his aggressive acts were committed prior to the victim's death. She and the others lasted a long time before dying from the repeated attacks or his frenzied, fantasy finale."

"OK, that's a bit vivid but a very interesting signature style." CB frowned. "Now about the timing thing, I mean, his getting better?"

"Refinements. The ligature marks from the devices he's using to control, restrain, and torture his victims. Those things have been changing. So much so that a body found two weeks ago, Agent Douglas and the clan are refusing to consider the latest victim." Tru shook her head in annoyance.

"Why? Where was she found?"

"Same general area. Near one of the tributaries leading into the Blue River. Some guy was walking his dog. Anyway, the victim was identified as a known prostitute. She's about ten years older than most of the other victims, tall, rawboned woman, and overdyed hair. What was interesting is that she was clothed, not partially nude like the others, and he had brought back the large handbag she must have been carrying the night he hijacked her," Tru recounted from the report.

"So why don't they think she's connected?"

"She's older, he dressed her back up, and he's using handcuffs now. I swear, though, it's the same type of slashing, mutilation, and restraint placements. I think he's just spent some money to add a bit of polish to his style and murder shack," Tru insisted. "I think she was available. She might not have been exactly what he wanted that night, but he likes his work, and any port in the storm . . . or something like that." Tru shrugged.

"What are you going to do about it?"

"Not much I can do but shout at the wind. I can't make them listen. I can't make anyone do anything. Either I have to become more persuasive or find some conclusive evidence that FBI Agent Mr. Jurist Doctorate from the University of Delaware is willing to buy," Tru said sourly.

"Is that jealously rearing its ugly little head?" CB asked.

"Maybe, and a bit of envy. Some of us don't have the luxury of opportunities that are available," Tru commiserated with herself. She looked through the swirling, heated steam of the hot tub and saw CB's eyebrow raised in concern. "Oh, all right," Tru said and then laughed. "I suppose if I really wanted to go back to school, I could. I do have a B.A., you know?"

"I know that, Tru. I don't think it's school you're complaining about. I think it's the fact that he's set in his mond and, without the specialized training he claims to have, he's set in his mind and there's nothing you can do about changing it. The real question is, what are you going to do with what you know based on your expertise and training? That's your focus, isn't it?" CB offered the question in earnest.

"I'm going to write the report like the good agent insisted. I'll hand-carry Lieutenant Haines a copy myself. It's not a contest. People are dying. I'll try to make a case to stay on the squad and be a little more useful as I get to feeling better," Tru said, sighing heavily.

"Sometime, hanging in there is the best any of us can do," CB said.

"I can be tenacious," Tru mumbled sourly.

"Good, then why don't you come over here and be tenacious with me?"

"I never let a lady ask twice." Tru grinned mischievously. "I think my back is feeling better, too."

"Great," CB crooned. "Now, let's see how well you are coming along in your process of rejuvenation."

Tru felt a flush of anticipation as she took CB into her arms.

As their lips touched, pulling them forward into each other's water-heated bodies, the phone on the wrought-iron table rang.

"We could ignore it," CB suggested as she felt Tru's lips tense against her mouth.

"I can't do that," Tru said apologetically as she reached for the phone. She put the phone to her ear. "Who's calling and what do you want?"

"Tru, it's my apartment . . . you gave them the number?" CB shook her head at Tru and laughed.

CB heard a jumbled, one-sided discussion. "What murder? Where? Temporary reassignment? Like hell, you say. What do you mean I'm transportation? What about my half-day work hours you insisted on? All right. All right, I'll leave first thing in the morning," Tru said as she slammed the phone back down on the table in anger.

"What?"

"Lieutenant Haines. I've been reassigned to do some damn transport duty. Seems as though some of our distant inmates have been involved in a murder. I can't believe this crap," Tru protested.

# Chapter 16

Detective Tru North reported to Lieutenant Haines by eight o'clock sharp the next morning. She carried with her the rough draft of the serial murderer analysis that she had promised to deliver. She waited as patiently as she could in a chair outside the lieutenant's office. It was nine before the lieutenant finally opened his door and waved her into the room.

Tru noticed that the lieutenant's forehead was creased into a deep frown. Tru sat down in a chair opposite him, letting the report rest on her knees and waiting to hear what the problems were. She hoped her disagreements with Agent Douglas were not going to be brought up.

"We've got a situation, detective," he began. "I've been on the phone since six this morning."

"You mentioned there had been a murder involving inmates originally transported from Jackson County Jail," Tru prompted.

"That's right. They've got a real mess down there in Chimney Rock. Two people are dead — a jailer and a female inmate. There may have been a witness. Seems as though one of the inmates, another woman, did not flee with the rest. That's where you come in," Haines said, raising his eyes from the jotted notes on his desk to meet Tru's gaze.

"Why I'm transporting?"

"Yes. The county attorney wants us to retrieve that inmate. Bring her back up here and put her in protective custody until this thing gets sorted out. The county attorney for Chimney Rock has agreed. On the surface, the way it looks, he's going to have his hands full investigating the incident and investigating the operational workings at the jail that allowed this to happen."

Tru shifted in the chair to relieve the cramping in her back that was beginning to annoy her. She was not wearing her back support, and she suspected that she should put on the light Velcro wrap the doctor had given her if she was going to be driving for hours to get to the Chimney Rock Jail.

"It does sound like a mess," Tru said. "I'm not objecting, but just why do you want me to transport this inmate back? Doesn't the Jackson County Jail

163

have transport units who do this sort of thing all the time?"

"Yes, it does. But they are not scheduled to go to that area for another week. Our county attorney does not want the female inmate in there that long, and the Jackson County sheriff's office as the original transport group are part of the problem right now. Additionally, if the inmate has information about the murders, or about the jail operations that allowed these murders to take place, she is going to be a source of suspicion and provocation for the sheriff and his deputies. She may be able to point fingers, or she could end up being targeted by them. Our county attorney is very likely going to have his hands full trying to explain to the dead female inmate's family or the ACLU why we transported someone into a fatal situation. Deep pockets and litigation are at stake. We want you to interview her on the way back. Find out what you can. You're not just transport. We need answers to this mess. I gave the man my word that I would send my best investigator. I think you're that person. That's why you're going to go get her and bring her back before this gets worse," Haines advised.

"Even after Agent Douglas has bent your ear?" Tru interjected.

Lieutenant Haines cocked his head sideways at Tru's question. He wondered how she had guessed that Agent Douglas had been in contact with him about their differences of opinion regarding the Blue River Stalker. He let a grin cross his face in response to her intuition. "Yes, detective. It would seem that the agent and I may have a different opinion as to the usefulness of disagreements. If you leave the report and analysis that you are clutching in your hand,"

164

Haines said, pointing at the papers Tru held, "I'll give it a fair reading, and we can talk about it after you get back."

"I'd appreciate that."

"Good. Now, I promised the county attorney you'd have the inmate back here this evening. I want you to take her immediately to the protective custody unit at the Jackson County Jail and to have a report on anything you can get from her on my desk tomorrow morning. Can you do that for us?"

"No problem," Tru said as she started to rise from the chair. "I was wondering, however, how the good agent was going to take my temporary reassignment?"

"He will have to be adult about it. Do you think he'll miss you for a day or two?"

"Probably not." Tru chuckled, although she tried not to.

"Frankly, the closest thing to action that group has seen was when you caught that guy who was trying to off his wife. He wasn't our Blue River Stalker, but it was a nice try on your part. Would have been a great try if you hadn't had to go on sick leave for all those weeks. And by the way, the half-day worker's compensation is killing me," he said with a grin. " 'Sides, it seems like our stalker is off his schedule. Let's hope he's moved on."

"They usually don't quit while they're still winning," Tru said, turning to leave.

"And North," Haines said, as she reached the door to his office. "Whether you win this argument with the special agent or not, do you want to stick with it or be reassigned back to the unit here?"

Tru stopped with her hand on the door handle. She considered the lieutenant's question for an instant. "Whatever you think is right, lieutenant. I don't like to quit a thing once I start, it but I don't care for lose-lose situations, either. I can handle whatever you need to have done," Tru responded.

"That's what I'm counting on. This little light-duty assignment is just what you need. Transport does not violate your doctor's orders, does it?" Haines asked.

"Ten to twelve hours of driving? Nah. I'm sure that's what she had in mind when she insisted on light duty," Tru responded sarcastically. She yearned for the soothing comforts of CB and the hot tub.

Tru North left the office, stopped by her desk to get her tiny tape-recording unit, and headed for the motor pool to secure a car for transporting her prisoner.

It was a long and anxious drive to the Chimney Rock Jail. The drive out of Kansas City, Missouri, on I-70 posed few problems, but the moment Tru exited the interstate to begin the drive to the Lake of the Ozarks, the roadway conditions rapidly deteriorated. December was in the process of lacing the highways with snow and ice. County crews were out scraping and sanding the narrow two-lanes as quickly as they could but they were fighting a losing battle. Heavy, gray clouds darkened the day and delivered dense swirling snows.

The two-lane road twisted, turned, and climbed over the rolling countryside. Snowplows, sand trucks, and anxious traffic crawled along in front of her, forcing Tru to be ever vigilant. Her hands tensed and untensed under the constant demands to keep her car from sliding into a ditch or into oncoming traffic. The hours snailed by.

The four-hour drive she had expected stretched interminably in front of her. As she left the southern outskirts of Jefferson City, she glanced at the clock on the dashboard. It read two in the afternoon, and she gloomily realized that four hours of driving had only gotten her a little better than halfway to her destination.

Tru pulled into the parking lot of the Chimney Rock Jail at six-thirty in the evening. It had been dark for two hours. As she got out of the car, Tru noted that the snow had let up slightly. She hoped she would be able to get her prisoner quickly and begin the long drive back as swiftly as possible.

As she walked through the sheriff's department door, Tru noticed the spit-and-polished Missouri Highway Patrol sergeant sitting behind the high wooden barrier of the department's complaint counter. The sergeant looked at her and smiled.

"You must be the detective from Kansas City," he said smoothly.

"You must be psychic," Tru countered as pleasantly as she could manage in her wearied state.

"Not hard to figure. Most folks around here dress a bit more casually," he noted, nodding at her. He had taken her in instantly as she walked through the door. The long, black wool coat did not hide the fine weave of the dark gunmetal jacket and pants, the tailored dark green silk blouse, or the expensive-looking black boots on her feet. It was smart clothing, but in Chimney Rock he knew that the locals were more prone to wearing jeans, bulky sweaters, sensible and inexpensive snow boots, and down-filled jackets. It did not take a rocket scientist to see that the visitor was not from around the county.

"I'm Detective North," she said as she pulled her identification badge and commission card case from her pocket. She placed it on the counter for him to officially acknowledge. "Is the sheriff here?"

"No, ma'am, and probably won't be for some time. Matter of fact, the whole department, what there is of it, has been suspended pending the investigation. Considering what's happened, and the fact that it looks as we have three murderers at large. That's why I'm here. Highway patrol is going to be standing in until the county attorney has finished his investigation. Emergency powers and emergency cooperation between agencies, if you know what I mean," he said advisingly.

"You haven't got an escape route on them or any sightings of them since this situation went down?"

"No. They stole the jailer's van. The one they killed. Our best guess is that they just drove out of town somewhere between eight last evening and four this morning. Frankly, I'm hoping they tried to get across an ice-covered bridge and we find them in the bottom of the lake next spring," the sergeant asserted.

"Sounds right to me," Tru agreed. "Seems like you all are in the middle of quite a mess."

"Would you like to see your prisoner?" he asked noncommittally.

"Is she ready?" Tru responded, hearing his evasion and shifting gears.

"Ready? You don't mean to try to take her back tonight, do you?"

"Those are my orders. With the condition of the roads, I don't want to have to be here any longer than necessary," Tru said.

"Well, it's your neck," he conceded and waved Tru back behind the counter. "Let's go see how your rider is doing."

Tru North followed the sergeant back down the short corridor, past the sheriff's department offices, past the cordoned-off dispatch room, and toward a small cell block.

"Your ride is here," he called into the cell as he placed the keys in the door. There was no response from the shadowed figure in the cell. "Grab your jacket and come on out."

The woman stood, reached for a jacket hanging on the back of a cell chair, walked into the lighted hallway, and stood blinking.

"You're taking me back to Kansas City?" Valerie said as she noticed the woman standing behind the sergeant.

"If you're Valerie Blake, I am. I'm Detective North," Tru responded evenly.

"I'm glad to see you," the young woman said as a tear slipped down her face.

"I think I can understand that," Tru said. She took the handcuffs from her pants belt and motioned for the woman to turn around.

"Could you cuff me in front? I promise not to be any trouble," Valerie pleaded and looked to the sergeant for support.

"She's been very cooperative, and in my opinion I think she is probably very lucky not to have been killed when the men made their jailbreak," he said, turning to Tru.

"How's that?" Tru asked.

"They killed the other woman, you know. Blake here got lucky. Hid inside the evidence room after the shooting started in the dispatch office. Looks as though they tried to get at her, hammered the door to the evidence room pretty good. Probably the only reason they didn't get to her is they figured they were running out of time."

"But if the jailer was the only one here..." Tru began.

"He was," the sergeant interrupted. "But some resident was trying to call in for a deputy to come to her house. Something about a pack of wild dogs running across her fields and harassing her cattle. It's on the recording system. Real pissed when she couldn't raise anyone. Best we can figure is that the call came in after they killed the jailer. We figure they must have panicked, noticed Blake here was missing, tried to get to her, and then simply fled," he explained.

"When did you find the bodies?" Tru asked as she placed the cuffs on Valerie's wrists.

"After Blake felt safe enough to leave the evidence room. She called the sheriff at his house, didn't you?" he asked Valerie for agreement.

Valerie nodded at him and smiled quickly at the detective, who had placed the cuffs locked in front of her.

"How long was that?" Tru asked Valerie.

"I don't know. I was so afraid they were still out here. The room was pitch black and . . . I fell asleep. I don't know for how long. We'd been drinking . . ." Her voice trailed off.

"Alcohol?" Tru asked incredulously.

"Yeah . . ." Valerie said weakly. "It's a long story . . ."

"I've got time on the way back," Tru interrupted as she looked at her watch. There would be hours for talking available on the long road back.

"Anyway, she called and the sheriff raised us and every deputy he could muster. There's been an all-points bulletin out on the jailer's van and the men since four this morning. County officers and the highway patrol in a ten-county range are out looking for them. This weather doesn't help much. Lots of folks are busy trying to work accident scenes and more. The escapees could be anywhere, but then you know what I'm hoping for. As for your transport, our county attorney grilled Ms. Blake here until noon. He's pretty satisfied she didn't have anything to do with it," the sergeant advised.

"I see," Tru said.

"Where was the jailer and the other woman when you got here?" Tru asked the sergeant.

"Jailer was at the dispatch room, on the floor. He had two bullet holes in him. One in the chest and the other in the head. The woman, a firebug from Kansas City, was found in a cell on the men's block. Coroner said it appeared as though she had been raped before they finished her off. Looks as though she might. have died slow. No mercy shot to the head. They used a knife on her," the sergeant said, letting his voice trail off.

171

Tru glanced around, looked in the direction of the door leading to the dispatch office, and peered down the short hall leading to the men's cell block. "Where's that evidence closet?"

"Right over there," the sergeant said, pointing to a battered and scarred door ten feet back down the hallway they had traversed to get to the women's cell block. The evidence room was located around the corner and four feet south of the dispatch office.

Tru North looked at the inmate she was about to transport back to Kansas City, Missouri. "You must have seen and heard a great deal?"

"Too much," Valerie responded between trembling lips.

"Sergeant," Tru began. "I know we'll have the cooperation of the highway patrol if I ask that copies of the investigative report, autopsies, and crime-scene photos are sent to the Jackson County attorney."

"That would be my understanding," he responded.

"Good. Then I have only one more question before we take off. Can you tell me if there's any quicker way I can get back to Kansas City without having to go to Jeff City first?" Tru asked.

"You bet. But let's get a map so I can show you. The only way out of here is on a two-lane. You won't hit the four-lane until you come to I-70. However, I think we might be able to shave an hour or so off your drive," he responded, turning back toward the way they had come in. "I still think it's foolish to start before daylight."

"I appreciate your concern, sergeant, but I have my orders. I'm sure you know what that means."

"I do, but I also believe in flexibility," he countered.

"Me, too, but it's not an option," Tru said.

Fifteen minutes later, Tru and her prisoner walked out of the sheriff's department in Chimney Rock and headed for the vehicle. Tru placed her prisoner in the front passenger seat, tightened the seat belt around the woman, shut the door, and spent the next ten minutes cleaning the snow from the windows where it had piled. With her gloved hand wet and cold, Tru jumped back into the car, shivering. The car was cold, and she let the engine idle until the defroster began to have an effect on the snowy windshield. She wanted to make sure that she could see the roadway and be comfortable as much as possible on the long drive home.

Tru checked the map the sergeant had given her and the notes she had taken regarding his advised route. She pulled the car out of the parking lot and across the street to a gas station. She did not want to chance running out of gas on any long dark stretch of road in the forested heart of the Lake of the Ozarks. After filling the tank with gas, Tru and her prisoner were headed north along Highway 7 on the route the highway patrol sergeant had promised would be a quicker way home.


The black van waited ten minutes before pulling out of the alleyway. Jeffery Lahee snorted at the continued rewards his patience and perseverance provided him.

# Chapter 17

"Are you warm enough?" Tru asked her passenger in an attempt to distract herself from the tension of the dark and snowy road. The last forty miles had been a constant, hard task of trying to see through the swirling snow, to keep the faint, snow-blown yellow line in sight, and to anticipate the curves of the unfamiliar roadway. The white-knuckled effort caused Tru's hands to ache. The constant vigilance was making her tense. It felt like tiny, sharp electrodes were racing up and down the tender nerve pathways of her back. She had no idea where they were other than that they were heading along a long strip of blacktop that would lead to Highway 50 and then on to I-70. The trees overhanging the road with their knurled, leaf-stripped skeletal limbs, looked like petrified giants threatening to seize the car. Her imagination was working overtime.

"Yeah. I'm fine," Valerie Blake finally responded, and she fell silent again.

"That's not going to do. You're going to have to help me stay awake. The snow in the headlights is mesmerizing," Tru urged.

"What do you want me to do?"

"Let's try having a conversation. I know the state troopers have already talked to you, but why don't you tell me what happened back there?"

"Why?"

Tru glanced momentarily at her passenger, wondering if the female prisoner's part in the murders was as innocent as she had led the highway patrol officers to believe. The reluctance in the sharp response caused some alarm bells to go off in Tru's head.

"Well, let's say that hauling you back up to Kansas City is only part of my job. The other part is finding out what happened. I'm not going to be the last person to talk to you, and when I get back my boss is going to be expecting some answers. Then again, maybe you saw or heard something that will give us some clues as to where the men may have run to," Tru explained.

"I hope you catch them. What they did was awful. John didn't deserve to . . . to die like that," Valerie choked.

"You knew John, liked him?"

"He was a nice man. Treated me real good. Treated everyone good."

"How so?"

Valerie sniffed and reached awkwardly into her jacket pocket for a used Kleenex. "He brought us stuff."

"Like what?"

"He brought in ice cream and he would stop at a restaurant on his way in to get us barbecue. He talked to me, talked to all of us, like we were real people. Like we counted, instead of just being inmates."

"Did he buy this stuff himself? Why do you think he did that?"

"He bought the ice cream, and the other stuff came out of our dollar-a-day wages for working at the jail. He wasn't trying to get anything from us, if that's what you are thinking," Valerie asserted pointedly.

"OK, so he was a nice guy. How did you and the other prisoners get out of your cells that night?" Tru asked as she slowed the car to make a hairpin curve in the road. She looked at the speedometer and realized that at 15 miles per hour she and her passenger would be lucky to see Kansas City, Missouri, before sunrise.

"We'd been out most of the day. We were cleaning and fixing up the place," Valerie began.

"All of you were trustee status?"

"Yeah. That was the sheriff's idea. I had volunteered for it first, but I guess he figured that having five people working instead of just one would get the job done a lot faster."

"What went wrong with his idea?" Tru asked, turning to look at the young woman.

Valerie looked at Tru as a heavy sigh passed her lips. "The idea. It was wrong. I'd been at the jail for weeks. That bunch, the four of them, Jeff, Dawn, Dave, and Flipper, were new. Flipper was local. He'd busted up some bar. The other was from Jackson County, like me. I think Flipper was related to John somehow, cousin, two or three times removed," Valerie recalled. She fidgeted uneasily in the seat of the car. "I thought the people the jail sent out weren't supposed to be dangerous."

"Me, too," Tru mumbled in agreement. "Problem with that classification system is, even if the rap sheet says someone is a nonviolent felon," Tru responded, feeling the same discontent Valerie was expressing, "it never indicates what someone might do or be capable of doing if they have a reason, or if there's something about them even the police don't know."

"What you don't know can hurt you."

"Exactly. So was that it? Did they suddenly decide to take advantage of the fact that John was alone? Do you think they had intended to rape and murder both of you, you and Dawn, that is?" Tru asked, noticing the distant lights of a car rounding the bend in the road she had recently had trouble navigating. She smirked at the lights, wondering how to feel about the fact that she was not the only fool trying to drive in the mid-winter blizzard. She quickly returned her eyes to the blackened roadway. *You're on your own*, she thought, glancing back at the sweep of headlights.

"It had been going on all week. John would let us out in the evening after we had supper. We'd go get the mops, paint, or buffer, or whatever we needed to fix up at the jail. Dave and Jeff had been sniffing around Dawn all that time. And Dawn, she didn't help herself much, except she wanted to help herself to both or all of them. She flirted. A lot. I had seen her rubbing up to Jeff when Dave wasn't looking and coming on to Dave when Jeff was somewhere else. She was just that way, I guess," Valerie speculated.

"Some can be. If everything had been going on that way for some time . . ." Tru's voice drifted off. "What makes you think that night ended so differently?"

Valerie sat quietly in her corner of the seat. She turned her face to the window and watched the dark and gloomy trees rush by her window. The swirling of the snow disappeared into the dark at the front edge of the bumper, reminding her how out of control her life had become. Everything she had ever thought about changing or wanted to change was disappearing from the light and into the black night.

Tru listened to the widening silence between them. She waited, giving Valerie a chance to gather her thoughts and arrive at a need to tell the truth she knew.

"It was the beer."

"Beer? The jailer brought beer?" Tru heard her voice respond in surprise.

"No, not John, some other deputy. But they didn't bring it to us. Dave found a whole bunch and a bottle of bourbon under some deputy's desk. We figured he must have taken it off someone, don't know whom. Probably some kids. Anyway, Dave was cleaning the room, and there it was."

"When was this?"

" 'Bout ten or ten-thirty. John had come on around nine. He usually stayed with us and dispatched until six or seven in the morning. He was pretty tired last night when he came to work."

"Go on," Tru encouraged Valerie when she turned her head again to stare out into the dark.

"He fell asleep. Sat there in the big old comfortable chair in the dispatch office and fell asleep. We'd seen him do it before. 'Cept this night we had a lot of beer to entertain ourselves with. I drank, too."

"I figured as much," Tru offered softly. She had read the arrest and incarceration reports of each of the inmates from Kansas City before leaving the office. There was not enough in any of the files to provide an answer as to why a group of nonviolent offenders would turn on each other or turn to murder. The mixture of alcohol could be the missing key.

"Did you tell the highway patrol officers about the beer?"

"No," Valerie whispered. "We took our empties out to the Dumpster inside the sally port as we finished each one. Ha!" Valerie suddenly laughed.

The sudden outburst half startled Tru. She had not expected the sharpness of the laugh in the close confines of the car. A flashing sweep of light caught her attention in the rearview mirror, and she looked up to see the lights of the vehicle behind her appear to be closing the distance between them. *Idiot*, Tru declared in judgment to herself as she watched the lights drawing closer. Whoever he was, Tru felt certain that he had no more reason to hurry on the windswept snowy night than she did. *Accident waiting to happen.* She shrugged and returned her attention to the road and Valerie.

"You think that's funny?" Tru asked.

"I think it's funnier than shit that we were so worried about cleaning up after ourselves. I think it's funny that we thought the deputy would not notice or that we wouldn't get into trouble..."

"You didn't expect to get by with it, did you?"

"No, not really. I knew we wouldn't, and I figure they finally realized they wouldn't get by with it, either." Valerie sighed.

"So if John was killed to keep him quiet, why do you think they killed Dawn and then wanted to kill you?"

"I think it was the other way around. I told you Dawn had been messin' around with coming on to both Jeff and Dave. I think after everybody got a bit lubricated with the beer, she made them an offer neither one would refuse. Then maybe she didn't, maybe they just had all the tease they could stand and decided that she was going to have to put up or shut up. Hell, I don't know. I wasn't there," Valerie declared vehemently.

"Where were you then?"

"Minding my own business and trying to keep out of sight so none of those guys would get the wrong idea. I don't like men that way. I don't care for men at all, if you know what I mean," Valerie flatly stated.

"I think I get the picture. But you didn't answer my question. Where were you?" The file report from the social worker had indicated that Valerie was a sister with a major alcohol problem. Young, lost, and heading down the wrong road; there was little or nothing Tru could do to help her.

"Last time I went to the sally port, I stayed there. I sat and drank the last three beers I had with me. I didn't want any trouble. I didn't want to know what they were up to, and I certainly didn't want to have to listen to or see straight sex. I sat there, drank, and thought. I hoped everything would somehow simply be all right or go away."

"How long was that? How long did you sit out in the sally port?"

"A long time. Maybe an hour or more. I got real cold. It's not heated as much out there. I wrapped myself in pile of old, thin quilts we had been using as drop cloths for the painting. I drifted off a bit, I think, and then woke up when I heard the shot."

"When they were killing John?"

"I guess. I went running back inside. I have no idea what I was thinking. I got to just outside the dispatch office and saw Jeff standing over John. He'd shot him in the chest, but John was still alive. Flipper, the little guy who was supposed to be his cousin, was saying, "Shoot him again, Jeff. Do it again.' " She choked.

"What did you do?"

"Nothing. I didn't do a thing. I could not think; I could not move. All I did was stand there until I saw Jeff raise the gun and point it at John again. That's when I finally moved. I ran back to my cell. Like an idiot. I don't know what I was going to do or how those bars would keep me from getting shot. I just ran. When I got to the cell, I started to reach for the bars . . . there was blood . . . and then I saw her . . ." Valerie's voice trailed off. "Those bastards had tied her up, cut her throat, and cut her all around her private parts."

"Then . . ." Tru gently prompted.

"Then I ran. As fast as I could. I wanted out of there. I figured I was next. I ran back toward the dispatch office. I couldn't get out of the building through the sally port, and I knew my only chance was out through the front doors. God, I was scared . . ."

"You didn't have many options," Tru said.

"I stopped 'cause I didn't want them to see me. They were inside arguing whether or not to shoot John again. So I tried to slip past the door while they weren't looking. But he saw me . . . Jeff looked up as he crouched over John and saw me. His eyes, his eyes went wild and crazy, and then he pulled the trigger while he had the muzzle pointed at John's head. That was when I knew I couldn't make the door."

"So you hid in the evidence room instead." Tru finished Valerie's sentence.

"It was all I could think of. It has a metal door. I was hoping, I guess, that if I got inside and locked it, they might not be able to shoot me, too." The tears streamed down Valerie's face. She blew her nose noisily into a second Kleenex.

"Or worse. You were very lucky." Tru slowed the car down as she rounded a bend and discovered a slow-moving snowplow lumbering down the road. Exasperated, Tru tapped the brakes to further slow the speed of her vehicle and dropped the automatic clutch slowly into low gear. She looked into the rearview mirror and noticed that the dark vehicle with its bright lights was directly behind her now. In annoyance she flipped the rearview mirror up into the headliner to get the reflected glare out of her eyes. "Asshole," Tru muttered.

"What?" Valerie was startled.

"Not you. This idiot behind us. If he gets any closer, I'm going to have to ask him to go steady," Tru quipped.

Valerie laughed. She laughed at Tru's remark until her eyes began to fill with a different kind of tears.

The ploy had worked. Tru had intentionally wanted to break the tension because she had more questions she intended to ask Valerie Blake. There was something, some kind of question rattling around at the back of her mind, and she wanted to find out what it was. An inkling skated near her consciousness but then skimmed away.

"Tell me about the way Dawn was tied up and about the cuts, if you can?" Tru asked.

"Why do you want to know about that?" Valerie asked in surprise.

"I don't know just yet, but how she was injured is important. Try to help me understand what happened. You can appreciate how important it is to get these guys. The details are part of understanding how to find them," *I think.* Tru questioned her own motives for insisting that Valerie be as vivid in her recall as she could.

"I glanced at her. It was horrible. Sick bastards."

"I know . . . please try . . ."

"She was lying partly on her side. I could see that they used a pair of handcuffs, I guess one of them found them in the deputy's office. Then, like that wasn't enough, they wrapped masking tape around and around her head, covering her mouth and eyes. I

183

don't get it. I just don't get it. I mean, she had been offering herself to both of them, hell, all of them, by what I could tell. Why the hell did they have to do that to her?" Valerie angrily shouted the question.

"I don't know, Valerie. I don't know. Maybe it's because some people like those sorts of things, or maybe whatever you and I can imagine, it would never be right. We don't see the world they see. Thank the goddess for that. Can you tell me about the knife wounds?"

"No, not really. I didn't look. They had cut her though . . . down here," Valerie said, pointing to her pelvic region. "That's where most of the blood was . . . there and at her throat," she whispered.

"Hmm." Tru frowned. The snowplow in front of her car slowed to a crawl and turned off to the darkened side street of a small town. As the headlights of her car swept ahead, she saw a tiny black-on-white sign declare her entrance into the outskirts of Climax Springs, Missouri. She laughed as she drove past the sign. "Did you see that?" Tru asked, turning to look at Valerie. "Never mind. I was amused at some of the names people come up with for their communities. Like that one back there. I know a few people who would be amused to get a letter postmarked with that name," she continued. Tru's car passed under the one streetlight and through the five-block town.

"OK, if you say so," Valerie responded distractedly. "Are you hungry?"

"Now that you mention it, I think I am. Maybe we can find a town that doesn't roll its streets up after eight around here. One thing for sure, coffee would be in order if I'm going to stay awake on this little hike."

The road twisted into the night. After a few minutes, Tru noticed that the flakes that had been falling all afternoon had become thicker, fatter, and wetter as they hit the windshield. A change in weather was coming, and the new moisture would fall on the already hard packed snow.

Tru looked behind her, using the outside mirror. She was disappointed to see that the vehicle that had been behind her for the last fifty miles had not turned off at Climax Springs. As she increased her speed, the vehicle drifted farther behind her. *Eat my snow.* Tru grinned mischievously at the receding lights.

# Chapter 18

The road had darkened into the rolling hills and thick-forested roadside the moment they left the single streetlight of Climax Springs. Tru gave her concentration to the road and let Valerie lapse into a thoughtful silence.

Tru had more questions to ask, but they could wait. Tru felt numb and tired from the exhaustion of the drive. Her nerves pulled at her shoulders and maltreated back. A cup of coffee, a bowl of soup, and a sandwich sounded like an excellent idea. She hoped the next town would be larger and open for business.

Stabbing bright car lights suddenly flooded the inside of the car. Alarmed, Tru grabbed at the rear-view mirror and jerked it into its proper place. Round glowing headlights grew in alarming proportion and abruptly covered the face of the mirror.

In the same instant, the vehicle slammed into the rear of her car. Valerie screamed as Tru fought for control of the vehicle. The collision sent her car careening and spinning on the snow-packed highway. In less time than she could blink in surprise, Tru watched in slow-motion helplessness as the car bounced, quaked, and swung wildly over a ridge and into the blackness of a pit. The undercarriage slammed the boulders as the car shuddered and twisted into the air.

"Ah, shit," Tru shouted. The car rolled on its side down the hill, swinging its rear end around wildly until it collided with an ancient oak. Valerie's screams rang in her ears.

In the sudden, shattering silence, Tru hung upside down in her seat belt amid the smothering plastic of the quickly deflating air bag, trying to take inventory of strains, broken bones, and bleeding. She was surprised to find that she was fine.

"Are you allright?" Tru called to Valerie as she struck at the passenger's air bag, punching it to find the young woman.

"Fine. But this seat belt is cutting me in two," she complained. "What the hell happened?"

"Some idiot driver. I think he tried to pass us and rammed us instead," Tru said as she found the seat belt fastener and released it. "Hold still and I'll get you down from there," Tru said as she located the release for Valerie's seat belt.

"Hold on," Tru said. Valerie fell to the roof and yelped in surprise. Tru had a hard time keeping herself from chuckling at the aggravation and absurdity of their predicament. She bit her lip. She was tired and realized that her sudden desire to giggle hysterically was from the combination of spent nerves and travel exhaustion.

"Can you get turned around and up?"

"Give me a minute. These handcuffs don't make maneuvering easy."

Tru sat on the windshield and fished into the pockets of her coat for her cellular phone. "Goddess, let there be someone out there in nine-one-one land," she prayed as she hit the green-lit numbers.

"Bowling Green County, nine-one-one. What's your emergency?" the dispatcher asked Tru. "We're pretty backed up tonight," he said as though his caller needed to qualify for an emergency response.

Tru heard the implication. "One, I'm at the bottom of a ravine about two miles west of some place called Climax Springs. Two, three, and four: I'm Detective North with the Kansas City Police Department. I'm transporting a prisoner. Do you think I qualify for a little help out here?" Tru chided.

"You say two miles west of Climax and you're a detective?" he asked, sounding a bit more attentive.

"Yes," Tru responded. A gunshot shattered the driver's side window. "Shit! I'm being shot at!" Tru said, ducking and quickly stuffing the cellular phone back into her coat pocket.

She grabbed Valerie by her jacket, pushed her, and crawled across her to the door. As she reached for the door handle, a second shot whipped in to ricochet off the rim of the front tire. Tru pitched open the door, shoved Valerie in front, and heard her fall screaming onto snow-covered boulders. Tru quickly tumbled out after her. Crawling across the cold, hard surface of the boulders, she found Valerie and pulled at her arm to help her get her on her feet. Tru's feet danced between slick stones and seemingly bottomless piles of snow as she fought the icy surfaces and sought safe purchase. She managed to get and keep herself and Valerie fairly upright long enough to totter downhill and through thickened brush. Stumbling and dashing headlong through the thicket while tugging at Valerie to keep pace, Tru stepped out into the open maw of the void.

Reflexively clutching Valerie's jacketed arm, Tru held on as they fell into the night. Through an eternity of milliseconds they plummeted down the bottom of the ravine. They came to rest at the ice-crusted water's edge.

"Thanks —"

"Shut up," Tru harshly whispered. She did not want to give the shooter a target in the dark. She pulled her 9 mm from her waistband and listened intently for the sounds of movement in the space above them. "Here," she murmured softly and put her left hand into Valerie's chilled fingers. The handcuff key dropped into Valerie's fingers.

In the dark, Valerie's eyes widened briefly, but she needed no further prompting to get to work on the locks of her handcuffs. Fear pounded deep in Valerie's chest. They might not make it back to Kansas City alive. She huddled close to the detective as she worked the key.

"Is he up there?" Valerie breathed in an anxious whisper.

Tru glanced upward, saw the thin glow of lights above, and leaned backward, straining to see if anyone was standing above and near them. She figured the glow was from the headlights of the car they had just abandoned, but nothing moved and no shadow crossed the luster. "I don't know, but we can't stay here," Tru said, trying to pull her feet from the cold, muddy water.

"You don't think they are gone now, do you?" Valerie hoped.

"Can't tell . . . I mean, I know there's road-rage in Kansas City, but I certainly didn't think it was prevalent in hill country," Tru mused, trying to make sense out of why someone who had obviously run them off the road would want to shoot them. She looked around the creek slopes, squinted across to where she thought the other side might be and down the banks on both sides. "Come on," she commanded, tugging at Valerie's freed arm as she crept along the bank.

Dead limbs and washed-up shattered tree trunks, large flat river rocks, and mounds of snow impeded their way. They climbed, crawled, and slipped under, through, and over the obstructions. Twigs and limbs snatched at their hair, clothing, and faces as they struggled along, hugging the high, slippery slope. Tru's hands were numbed in the cold, and the 9 mm felt like it weighed a hundred pounds. She found herself trying to remember to keep a tight grip and to keep her finger off the trigger.

It was slow going, but Tru was determined to get as far away from where they had been shot at as she could. She wanted some distance between them and the ruined police car before she poked her head over the embankment.

Behind Tru, Valerie grappled valiantly with the encumbrances. Tru could hear occasional grunts and quick, quiet cries of pain or alarm as the creek's wild debris snared and tore at Valerie. After stumbling along for what Tru could best estimate was close to a hundred feet, she discovered that the embankment suddenly dropped off. Pulling herself up and over the rise, Tru peered into the night. No sound came from the thinning tree line.

"Come on," she urged Valerie.

"Easy for you to say," Valerie groused as she slipped into the mud.

A slash of light appeared then suddenly disappeared through the dark ahead of Tru. She watched as it weaved closer and closer to where she had climbed over the bank. She crouched down and waited. The lights appeared again, and she could see the flashing red-and-blue lights rotating above the broad-beamed headlights of the highway patrol car.

"There's a highway over here," Tru said, turning back to get Valerie's attention.

"It's about time," Valerie cheered. Just then a shot rang out and the bullet slammed against the tree Tru was standing next to.

Valerie watched in horror as Tru's body jerked and fell hard to the ground. Valerie leaped and ducked away from where she believed the bullet had come.

She crawled to where Tru had fallen. The detective lay facedown in the snow.

"Detective!" Valerie hissed. She grabbed Tru's coat to pull her over.

Tru came up spitting and sputtering, her face and eyes covered with snow. "Shouldn't dive in snow," she whispered as she wiped the snow from her face. "Son of a bitch won't give up!"

"What do we do?" Valerie asked. Terror burned in her throat.

"We split up. You see those lights over there? Those car lights coming our direction?"

"Yes." Valerie nodded. The lights appeared to slip along the hill.

"Good. Go in that direction. Go as fast as you can. If we're lucky, that guy will be the first in a long line of police cars. Tell them where I am . . . Now go . . . ahhh . . ." Tru stumbled verbally and realized she had forgotten the woman's name. She felt the jet-black fissure of disorientation falling down on her from the winter sky. A chill ran through her body, and she hoped she didn't forget how to shoot.

"But . . . ?"

"Do it. I'm going to see if I can cool off Mr. Road Rage here. Go!" Tru commanded and shoved Valerie away.

Valerie crouched and sprinted as quickly as she could through the expanding clearing. She held her arms out in front of her hoping, to ward off clobbering branches and save herself from running headlong into trees she could barely detect. The searing cold rushed in and out of her chest as she barreled toward the direction of the road.

Tru heard Valerie crashing through the brush and said a quick prayer to the goddess to protect the young woman. As she turned her attention back toward the direction the shot came from, Tru heard the sound of a body sliding downhill. The soft swishing gave away her assailant's location.

She fired once, stood up, and ran wide around him toward her patrol car.

Her feet and legs cut deep into the piled snow as she continued to reel and lurch onward to where she hoped the law enforcement officers would be arriving. She stumbled down a drifting embankment and heard the sounds of brush snapping and mashing behind her. She lurched to her feet and fell behind a large boulder an instant before another shot rang out. From her crouched and shivering position, she hugged her body close to the boulder for protection.

"What the hell is wrong with you!" She screamed her demand for an answer from her predator.

For an answer, he fired two rapid shots at the face of the rock she hid behind. "Great," Tru muttered. "Now I suppose he's really pissed." Tru felt assured that whoever was after her was still under the impression that she and Valerie were traveling together. She tried to will the idea to her mind that Valerie was talking to a state trooper at that very moment and that a squadron of them would be descending on the idiot who seemed so intent on killing her.

From behind her, Tru could hear the sounds of cascading water and knew she must be close to some branch of the creek she had crossed. The idea of getting back into the water froze her mind, but she relented. Her choices were slim and none. She had to get away from him, and she had no idea if he was closing in or her or if he was waiting for her to give up.

Staying hunkered down, Tru jogged as quickly as she could toward the sound of the flowing water. An instant before she plunged over the edge, she recognized the sound, reached out, grabbed a tree limb, and swung precariously over the drop-off. Straining every muscle in her arm, she jerked herself backward to solid ground. The tumult of a cold, untamed river churned in unison to the roar of blood rushing and pounding in her ears. Her shoulder ached as though the muscles were on fire.

A sudden seizure in her back sent hot, anguished waves through her legs, and she tumbled to the ground, landing in a heap at the foot of the tree that had saved her life. "This isn't going well," she muttered. Tiny flashes of lights danced before her eyes.

"You can say that again," his reply came at her, high and to the left.

Tru heard the hammer on his gun click back.

Reflexively, Tru's arm snapped out in front of her. She fired three rapid shots and waited for the return exchange. The echo of her gunfire rattled along the tree-thickened riverbank and then silence.

Tru rolled over on the ground, pulled herself prone, and held her breath, tensing for any sounds of movement that might come her way.

Nothing but the sound of her own breath met her ears. She rolled over as best she could as a tingling numbness crawled up her legs. A few flakes of snow fell through the boughs of the evergreens and landed on her eyelashes. She blinked them away and looked through the branches at the moon that had begun to shine through the thinning snow clouds.

She smiled up at the face of the full moon, another manifestation of the goddess. "Nice we could get together this way," Tru commented. "I'm a little tired, Lady. I hope you don't take it personally if I lie here, look at you, and wait for whatever happens next," Tru said. She wrapped her coat over her and continued to gaze at the moon.

The moon was holding vigil, its light luminous on Tru's face, when they found her.

# Chapter 19

Dan Keeler shifted his eighteen-wheeler into a lower gear as he pulled around the sweeping wide bend on Highway 7. As his truck hunkered down and grabbed at the sloshing snow vanishing in the bright light of day, he checked the clock on the dashboard. It was ten-thirty. If he could get out of the Mark Twain Forest and down to Arkansas in the next three hours, he'd be home in Nashville before the day was through.

The glare of bright sun on the snow made his eyes water even through the shade of his sunglasses. He pulled the glasses roughly off his face and rubbed his eyes. For a moment he took his eyes off the road, and when he refocused he saw something stumble onto the roadway.

He jerked the steering wheel and fought for control of the big rig. Furiously tapping the brakes as he went, he glanced at the pale face as the right side of his truck flew past it. Instantly, cold sweat washed over him.

He braked, letting the hydraulics ease the rig to a stop. His hands gripped the wheel as the truck bounced to a stop on the narrow edge of the shoulder.

Dan opened his door and climbed out of the truck on shaking knees. He wanted to know what he had hit. If it was a deer, he'd make a point of calling someone on the CB radio, advising what the closest mile marker was so they could do whatever they wanted with it. If it was a human being and not his imagination, he decided not to think about that.

Dan looked into the culvert and off to the tree line. He thought about going down the short embankment, looking for blood in the snow or near the trees. But he decided he didn't want to know about anything that much. He kicked at a beer can that lay crushed on the roadbed and turned to leave.

"Can I get a ride?"

The sound of the voice made Dan's heart leap to the back of his teeth. He jumped, and stood holding his hand over his slamming heart.

"Could I catch a ride?" the young woman said as she walked out of the tree line.

"Christ on a crutch, hon!" Dan exclaimed. "What the hell are you doing out here?" he asked as he looked at the wet and bedraggled woman who limped toward him.

"I . . . I lost my ride," Valerie responded with a wry grin.

"That's a damn shame," Dan retorted in anger. He imagined that some man who was unhappy about the way the night was going had let the young woman out of a car.

"Yes," Valerie said as she fought her way up the embankment. "Give me a hand," she asked as she tried to pull herself up the sharp rise.

Dan reached out and took hold of the chilly, muddy hand. "You just tell me where the son-of-a-bitch went, and I'll make it right," he swore.

"No, that's fine. I'd just really like a ride," Valerie said, shooting anxious looks up and down the road.

"Where are you headed?" Dan asked, putting a cautious arm protectively around the shivering young woman. He walked her around to the passenger's side of his truck.

"Out of Missouri, anywhere," Valerie stated. "Where were you going?"

"Watch your step," he advised as he helped her climb into the cab. "Nashville."

"Sounds good to me," she said as he closed the door.

Dan Keeler climbed back into the cab of his truck and smiled lightly at the thoroughly miserable looking young woman. "That'd be a long way from home." He saw a wry smile gently touch her lips.

"Already am," she replied. "I'd like to get a fresh start. Maybe I could make something of this one."

"OK," Dan replied as he gunned the diesel. "You can crawl up into the sleeper if you have a mind to. Ya kinda look like you need some food and rest. Why don't you rest first, and after we cross over to Arkansas, we'll see about gettin' you some food."

"Deal," Valerie said as she turned to look at the sleeper bunk in the back of the cab. "I'm kind of . . ." She looked at her ruined clothes and dirty hands.

"Don't fret the dirt. You've had a bad time of it. All that will wash off. Go on and get some shut-eye. I won't bother you."

"I believe you," Valerie said as she crawled into the sleeper.

A couple miles down the road Dan watched two highway patrol cars top the hill ahead of him, their lights and sirens blazing as they shot past him headed in the direction he had traveled through. He had noticed that the highway had been simply lousy with cops this morning and figured that at the rate the troopers were going there had been a terrible accident.

He was glad he missed it.

# Chapter 20

"Where did they find her?" CB asked Major O'Donoghue. The phone call was the one she had been dreading. Tru had promised to come home the night before. There had been no word about her from anyone. Then the major had called and was trying to tell her what had happened.

"Some place called Climax Springs, near the spillway area they named the town after. Almost seems fitting," O'Donoghue offered gently.

"What's to be done?" CB asked.

"Well, seems as though that might be up to you. A sergeant from the highway patrol told me that she was asking if someone with a comfortable truck could come get her. Seems she's not anxious to wait until her car is towed or to ride in the cab of a tow truck."

"I can certainly understand that," CB responded, feeling her heart start to beat again.

"I gave her your telephone number."

"You did what?"

"Apparently, the stress of the adventure has given her a few blank spots in her memory again."

"I think she's going to have to take a break for a while. Either that or I am. I'm don't want her to have no memory at all."

"Think you can convince her of that?"

"I can be very persuasive, major. Trust me."

"Well, give her a call first. There're some loose ends she's trying to wrap up down there," Major O'Donoghue advised.

"Like what? What could be so important she's not ready to come home? I thought you said she wanted me to go get her?"

"I did. It's just that they haven't found the guy who was trying to kill her or her prisoner. Tru thinks she must have winged him. The county mounties and highway patrol are fairly certain he fell in and floated downstream. He managed to kill quite a few before Tru got him. They haven't found the other girl's body yet, either. Probably won't find either one of them until spring."

"I don't get it. How many people is he responsible for?"

"You'll have to get the details from Tru. But it appears he got two at the jail and his two escape buddies. They were found cut and trussed up in the back of the van he was driving. The trooper said Tru had the idea, because of the knife wounds and the way he tied his victims up, that the guy was the Blue River Stalker . . . can you imagine that?"

"Tru isn't one for jumping to conclusions as a form of exercise. When she's ready to make a move, she's usually got it planned out in advance."

"When doesn't she?"

"Good point. Although I have noticed that life has a way of surprising her every now and again. Anyway, I'll give her a call, but I'm heading down there this morning. She can just get that little bruised butt ready to come home," CB announced.

"Why don't you talk her into taking a bit of time, like a vacation, and stay in one of those cabins down there. Start getting Tru used to the idea of taking vacations?"

"That's an excellent idea. Would you watch Poupon while we're gone?"

"Say no more. See you when you get back," Major O'Donoghue said, signing off.

CB quickly changed clothes, packed a bag, and headed for the door. She would call Tru all right, but from the truck while she was on her way. CB had no intention of brooking any arguments.


At Tru's apartment the curious Poupon heard his mistress's phone ring and the answering device click on.

"Tru . . . this is Marki. I wanted to call and tell you I'm leaving the area next week. I'll be gone some time. I had some investments work out. I'm heading up to Montana for a long vacation. So . . . so anyway, I wanted to say good-bye, but I guess unless you get this before I leave, this will have to do instead. Don't worry about it . . . not everything in life ties up nice and neat. Take care of yourself and . . . you can even give CB my regards . . . love to you . . ."

The line went dead, and Poupon listened to the clicking and whirling of the message being saved on the machine. His curiosity satisfied, he walked over to the double French doors, scratched at the bottom of the one standing slightly ajar, and sauntered out into the day.

# LOOKING FOR NAIAD?

**Buy our books at**
**www.naiadpress.com**

**or call our toll-free number**
**1-800-533-1973**

**or by fax (24 hours a day)**
**1-850-539-9731**

SILVER THREADS by Lyn Denison.208 pp. Finding her way
back to love . . .                              ISBN 1-56280-231-3    $11.95

CHIMNEY ROCK BLUES by Janet McClellan. 224 pp. 4th Tru
North mystery.                                ISBN 1-56280-233-X    11.95

OMAHA'S BELL by Penny Hayes. 208 pp. Orphaned Keeley
Delaney woos the lovely Prudence Morris.    ISBN 1-56280-232-1    11.95

SIXTH SENSE by Kate Calloway. 224 pp. 6th Cassidy James
mystery.                                      ISBN 1-56280-228-3    11.95

DAWN OF THE DANCE by Marianne K. Martin. 224 pp. A dance
with an old friend, nothing more . . . yeah!    ISBN 1-56280-229-1    11.95

WEDDING BELL BLUES by Julia Watts. 240 pp. Love, family,
and a recipe for success.                    ISBN 1-56280-230-5    11.95

THOSE WHO WAIT by Peggy J. Herring. 160 pp. Two
sisters . . . in love with the same woman.    ISBN 1-56280-223-2    11.95

WHISPERS IN THE WIND by Frankie J. Jones. 192 pp. "If you
don't want this," she whispered, "all you have to say is 'stop.' "
                                               ISBN 1-56280-226-7    11.95

WHEN SOME BODY DISAPPEARS by Therese Szymanski.
192 pp. 3rd Brett Higgins mystery.          ISBN 1-56280-227-5    11.95

THE WAY LIFE SHOULD BE by Diana Braund. 240 pp. Which
one will teach her the true meaning of love?    ISBN 1-56280-221-6    11.95

UNTIL THE END by Kaye Davis. 256pp. 3rd Maris Middleton
mystery.                                      ISBN 1-56280-222-4    11.95

FIFTH WHEEL by Kate Calloway. 224 pp. 5th Cassidy James
mystery.                                      ISBN 1-56280-218-6    11.95

JUST YESTERDAY by Linda Hill. 176 pp. Reliving all the
passion of yesterday.                        ISBN 1-56280-219-4    11.95

THE TOUCH OF YOUR HAND edited by Barbara Grier and
Christine Cassidy. 304 pp. Erotic love stories by Naiad Press
authors.                                          ISBN 1-56280-220-8     14.95

WINDROW GARDEN by Janet McClellan. 192 pp. They discover
a passion they never dreamed possible.     ISBN 1-56280-216-X     11.95

PAST DUE by Claire McNab. 224 pp. 10th Carol Ashton
mystery.                                          ISBN 1-56280-217-8     11.95

CHRISTABEL by Laura Adams. 224 pp. Two captive hearts and
the passion that will set them free.          ISBN 1-56280-214-3     11.95

PRIVATE PASSIONS by Laura DeHart Young. 192 pp. An
unforgettable new portrait of lesbian love . . .    ISBN 1-56280-215-1     11.95

BAD MOON RISING by Barbara Johnson. 208 pp. 2nd Colleen
Fitzgerald mystery.                            ISBN 1-56280-211-9     11.95

RIVER QUAY by Janet McClellan. 208 pp. 3rd Tru North
mystery.                                          ISBN 1-56280-212-7     11.95

ENDLESS LOVE by Lisa Shapiro. 272 pp. To believe, once
again, that love can be forever.              ISBN 1-56280-213-5     11.95

FALLEN FROM GRACE by Pat Welch. 256 pp. 6th Helen Black
mystery.                                          ISBN 1-56280-209-7     11.95

THE NAKED EYE by Catherine Ennis. 208 pp. Her lover in the
camera's eye . . .                              ISBN 1-56280-210-0     11.95

OVER THE LINE by Tracey Richardson. 176 pp. 2nd Stevie
Houston mystery.                               ISBN 1-56280-202-X     11.95

JULIA'S SONG by Ann O'Leary. 208 pp. Strangely
disturbing . . . strangely exciting.          ISBN 1-56280-197-X     11.95

LOVE IN THE BALANCE by Marianne K. Martin. 256 pp.
Weighing the costs of love . . .              ISBN 1-56280-199-6     11.95

PIECE OF MY HEART by Julia Watts. 208 pp. All the
stuff that dreams are made of —               ISBN 1-56280-206-2     11.95

MAKING UP FOR LOST TIME by Karin Kallmaker. 240 pp.
Nobody does it better . . .                    ISBN 1-56280-196-1     11.95

GOLD FEVER by Lyn Denison. 224 pp. By author of *Dream
Lover.*                                          ISBN 1-56280-201-1     11.95

WHEN THE DEAD SPEAK by Therese Szymanski. 224 pp. 2nd
Brett Higgins mystery.                         ISBN 1-56280-198-8     11.95

FOURTH DOWN by Kate Calloway. 240 pp. 4th Cassidy James
mystery.                                          ISBN 1-56280-205-4     11.95

A MOMENT'S INDISCRETION by Peggy J. Herring. 176 pp.
There's a fine line between love and lust . . .    ISBN 1-56280-194-5     11.95

CITY LIGHTS/COUNTRY CANDLES by Penny Hayes. 208 pp.
About the women she has known . . .         ISBN 1-56280-195-3     11.95

POSSESSIONS by Kaye Davis. 240 pp. 2nd Maris Middleton
mystery.                              ISBN 1-56280-192-9      11.95

A QUESTION OF LOVE by Saxon Bennett. 208 pp. Every
woman is granted one great love.      ISBN 1-56280-205-4      11.95

RHYTHM TIDE by Frankie J. Jones. 160 pp.   . . . to desire
passionately and be passionately desired.   ISBN 1-56280-189-9      11.95

PENN VALLEY PHOENIX by Janet McClellan. 208 pp. 2nd
Tru North Mystery.                    ISBN 1-56280-200-3      11.95

BY RESERVATION ONLY by Jackie Calhoun. 240 pp. A
chance for true happiness.            ISBN 1-56280-191-0      11.95

OLD BLACK MAGIC by Jaye Maiman. 272 pp. 9th Robin
Miller mystery.                       ISBN 1-56280-175-9      11.95

LEGACY OF LOVE by Marianne K. Martin. 240 pp. Women
will do anything for her . . .        ISBN 1-56280-184-8      11.95

LETTING GO by Ann O'Leary. 160 pp. Laura, at 39, in love
with 23-year-old Kate.                ISBN 1-56280-183-X      11.95

LADY BE GOOD edited by Barbara Grier and Christine Cassidy.
288 pp. Erotic stories by Naiad Press authors.   ISBN 1-56280-180-5      14.95

CHAIN LETTER by Claire McNab. 288 pp. 9th Carol Ashton
mystery.                              ISBN 1-56280-181-3      11.95

NIGHT VISION by Laura Adams. 256 pp. Erotic fantasy romance
by "famous" author.                   ISBN 1-56280-182-1      11.95

SEA TO SHINING SEA by Lisa Shapiro. 256 pp. Unable to resist
the raging passion . . .              ISBN 1-56280-177-5      11.95

THIRD DEGREE by Kate Calloway. 224 pp. 3rd Cassidy James
mystery.                              ISBN 1-56280-185-6      11.95

WHEN THE DANCING STOPS by Therese Szymanski. 272 pp.
1st Brett Higgins mystery.            ISBN 1-56280-186-4      11.95

PHASES OF THE MOON by Julia Watts. 192 pp. . . . . hungry
for everything life has to offer.     ISBN 1-56280-176-7      11.95

BABY IT'S COLD by Jaye Maiman. 256 pp. 5th Robin Miller
mystery.                              ISBN 1-56280-156-2      10.95

CLASS REUNION by Linda Hill. 176 pp. The girl from her
past . . .                            ISBN 1-56280-178-3      11.95

DREAM LOVER by Lyn Denison. 224 pp. A soft, sensuous,
romantic fantasy.                     ISBN 1-56280-173-1      11.95

FORTY LOVE by Diana Simmonds. 288 pp. Joyous, heart-
warming romance.                      ISBN 1-56280-171-6      11.95

IN THE MOOD by Robbi Sommers. 160 pp. The queen of
erotic tension!                       ISBN 1-56280-172-4      11.95

SWIMMING CAT COVE by Lauren Douglas. 192 pp. 2nd
Allison O'Neil Mystery.               ISBN 1-56280-168-6      11.95

THE LOVING LESBIAN by Claire McNab and Sharon Gedan. 240 pp. Explore the experiences that make lesbian love unique.
ISBN 1-56280-169-4     14.95

COURTED by Celia Cohen. 160 pp. Sparkling romantic encounter.
ISBN 1-56280-166-X     11.95

SEASONS OF THE HEART by Jackie Calhoun. 240 pp. Romance through the years.
ISBN 1-56280-167-8     11.95

K. C. BOMBER by Janet McClellan. 208 pp. 1st Tru North mystery.
ISBN 1-56280-157-0     11.95

LAST RITES by Tracey Richardson. 192 pp. 1st Stevie Houston mystery.
ISBN 1-56280-164-3     11.95

EMBRACE IN MOTION by Karin Kallmaker. 256 pp. A whirlwind love affair.
ISBN 1-56280-165-1     11.95

HOT CHECK by Peggy J. Herring. 192 pp. Will workaholic Alice fall for guitarist Ricky?
ISBN 1-56280-163-5     11.95

OLD TIES by Saxon Bennett. 176 pp. Can Cleo surrender to a passionate new love?
ISBN 1-56280-159-7     11.95

LOVE ON THE LINE by Laura DeHart Young. 176 pp. Will Stef win Kay's heart?
ISBN 1-56280-162-7     11.95

DEVIL'S LEG CROSSING by Kaye Davis. 192 pp. 1st Maris Middleton mystery.
ISBN 1-56280-158-9     11.95

COSTA BRAVA by Marta Balletbo Coll. 144 pp. Read the book, see the movie!
ISBN 1-56280-153-8     11.95

MEETING MAGDALENE & OTHER STORIES by Marilyn Freeman. 144 pp. Read the book, see the movie!
ISBN 1-56280-170-8     11.95

SECOND FIDDLE by Kate 208 pp. 2nd P.I. Cassidy James mystery.
ISBN 1-56280-169-6     11.95

LAUREL by Isabel Miller. 128 pp. By the author of the beloved *Patience and Sarah.*
ISBN 1-56280-146-5     10.95

LOVE OR MONEY by Jackie Calhoun. 240 pp. The romance of real life.
ISBN 1-56280-147-3     10.95

SMOKE AND MIRRORS by Pat Welch. 224 pp. 5th Helen Black Mystery.
ISBN 1-56280-143-0     10.95

DANCING IN THE DARK edited by Barbara Grier & Christine Cassidy. 272 pp. Erotic love stories by Naiad Press authors.
ISBN 1-56280-144-9     14.95

TIME AND TIME AGAIN by Catherine Ennis. 176 pp. Passionate love affair.
ISBN 1-56280-145-7     10.95

PAXTON COURT by Diane Salvatore. 256 pp. Erotic and wickedly funny contemporary tale about the business of learning to live together.
ISBN 1-56280-114-7     10.95

INNER CIRCLE by Claire McNab. 208 pp. 8th Carol Ashton
Mystery.                                    ISBN 1-56280-135-X      11.95

LESBIAN SEX: AN ORAL HISTORY by Susan Johnson.
240 pp. Need we say more?                    ISBN 1-56280-142-2      14.95

WILD THINGS by Karin Kallmaker. 240 pp. By the undisputed
mistress of lesbian romance.                 ISBN 1-56280-139-2      11.95

THE GIRL NEXT DOOR by Mindy Kaplan. 208 pp. Just what
you d expect.                                ISBN 1-56280-140-6      11.95

NOW AND THEN by Penny Hayes. 240 pp. Romance on the
westward journey.                            ISBN 1-56280-121-X      11.95

HEART ON FIRE by Diana Simmonds. 176 pp. The romantic and
erotic rival of *Curious Wine*.              ISBN 1-56280-152-X      11.95

DEATH AT LAVENDER BAY by Lauren Wright Douglas. 208 pp.
1st Allison O'Neil Mystery.                  ISBN 1-56280-085-X      11.95

YES I SAID YES I WILL by Judith McDaniel. 272 pp. Hot
romance by famous author.                    ISBN 1-56280-138-4      11.95

FORBIDDEN FIRES by Margaret C. Anderson. Edited by Mathilda
Hills. 176 pp. Famous author's "unpublished" Lesbian romance.
                                             ISBN 1-56280-123-6      21.95

SIDE TRACKS by Teresa Stores. 160 pp. Gender-bending
Lesbians on the road.                        ISBN 1-56280-122-8      10.95

WILDWOOD FLOWERS by Julia Watts. 208 pp. Hilarious and
heart-warming tale of true love.             ISBN 1-56280-127-9      10.95

NEVER SAY NEVER by Linda Hill. 224 pp. Rule #1: Never get
involved with . . .                          ISBN 1-56280-126-0      11.95

THE WISH LIST by Saxon Bennett. 192 pp. Romance through
the years.                                   ISBN 1-56280-125-2      10.95

OUT OF THE NIGHT by Kris Bruyer. 192 pp. Spine-tingling
thriller.                                    ISBN 1-56280-120-1      10.95

LOVE'S HARVEST by Peggy J. Herring. 176 pp. by the author of
*Once More With Feeling*.                    ISBN 1-56280-117-1      10.95

THE COLOR OF WINTER by Lisa Shapiro. 208 pp. Romantic
love beyond your wildest dreams.             ISBN 1-56280-116-3      10.95

FAMILY SECRETS by Laura DeHart Young. 208 pp. Enthralling
romance and suspense.                        ISBN 1-56280-119-8      10.95

INLAND PASSAGE by Jane Rule. 288 pp. Tales exploring conven-
tional & unconventional relationships.       ISBN 0-930044-56-8      10.95

DOUBLE BLUFF by Claire McNab. 208 pp. 7th Carol Ashton
Mystery.                                     ISBN 1-56280-096-5      10.95

BAR GIRLS by Lauran Hoffman. 176 pp. See the movie, read
the book!                                    ISBN 1-56280-115-5      10.95

THE FIRST TIME EVER edited by Barbara Grier & Christine
Cassidy. 272 pp. Love stories by Naiad Press authors.

ISBN 1-56280-086-8    14.95

MISS PETTIBONE AND MISS McGRAW by Brenda Weathers.
208 pp. A charming ghostly love story.    ISBN 1-56280-151-1    10.95

CHANGES by Jackie Calhoun. 208 pp. Involved romance and
relationships.    ISBN 1-56280-083-3    10.95

FAIR PLAY by Rose Beecham. 256 pp. An Amanda Valentine
Mystery.    ISBN 1-56280-081-7    10.95

PAYBACK by Celia Cohen. 176 pp. A gripping thriller of romance,
revenge and betrayal.    ISBN 1-56280-084-1    10.95

THE BEACH AFFAIR by Barbara Johnson. 224 pp. Sizzling
summer romance/mystery/intrigue.    ISBN 1-56280-090-6    10.95

GETTING THERE by Robbi Sommers. 192 pp. Nobody does it
like Robbi!    ISBN 1-56280-099-X    10.95

FINAL CUT by Lisa Haddock. 208 pp. 2nd Carmen Ramirez
Mystery.    ISBN 1-56280-088-4    10.95

FLASHPOINT by Katherine V. Forrest. 256 pp. A Lesbian
blockbuster!    ISBN 1-56280-079-5    10.95

CLAIRE OF THE MOON by Nicole Conn. Audio Book —
Read by Marianne Hyatt.    ISBN 1-56280-113-9    16.95

FOR LOVE AND FOR LIFE: INTIMATE PORTRAITS OF
LESBIAN COUPLES by Susan Johnson. 224 pp.

ISBN 1-56280-091-4    14.95

DEVOTION by Mindy Kaplan. 192 pp. See the movie — read
the book!    ISBN 1-56280-093-0    10.95

SOMEONE TO WATCH by Jaye Maiman. 272 pp. 4th Robin
Miller Mystery.    ISBN 1-56280-095-7    10.95

GREENER THAN GRASS by Jennifer Fulton. 208 pp. A young
woman — a stranger in her bed.    ISBN 1-56280-092-2    10.95

TRAVELS WITH DIANA HUNTER by Regine Sands. Erotic
lesbian romp. Audio Book (2 cassettes)    ISBN 1-56280-107-4    16.95

CABIN FEVER by Carol Schmidt. 256 pp. Sizzling suspense
and passion.    ISBN 1-56280-089-1    10.95

THERE WILL BE NO GOODBYES by Laura DeHart Young. 192
pp. Romantic love, strength, and friendship.    ISBN 1-56280-103-1    10.95

FAULTLINE by Sheila Ortiz Taylor. 144 pp. Joyous comic
lesbian novel.    ISBN 1-56280-108-2    9.95

OPEN HOUSE by Pat Welch. 176 pp. 4th Helen Black Mystery.

ISBN 1-56280-102-3    10.95

ONCE MORE WITH FEELING by Peggy J. Herring. 240 pp.
Lighthearted, loving romantic adventure.    ISBN 1-56280-089-2    11.95

FOREVER by Evelyn Kennedy. 224 pp. Passionate romance — love
overcoming all obstacles.                 ISBN 1-56280-094-9     10.95

WHISPERS by Kris Bruyer. 176 pp. Romantic ghost story.
                                          ISBN 1-56280-082-5     10.95

NIGHT SONGS by Penny Mickelbury. 224 pp. 2nd Gianna
Maglione Mystery.                         ISBN 1-56280-097-3     10.95

GETTING TO THE POINT by Teresa Stores. 256 pp. Classic
southern Lesbian novel.                   ISBN 1-56280-100-7     10.95

PAINTED MOON by Karin Kallmaker. 224 pp. Delicious
Kallmaker romance.                        ISBN 1-56280-075-2     11.95

THE MYSTERIOUS NAIAD edited by Katherine V. Forrest &
Barbara Grier. 320 pp. Love stories by Naiad Press authors.
                                          ISBN 1-56280-074-4     14.95

DAUGHTERS OF A CORAL DAWN by Katherine V. Forrest.
240 pp. Tenth Anniversay Edition.    ISBN 1-56280-104-X          11.95

BODY GUARD by Claire McNab. 208 pp. 6th Carol Ashton
Mystery.                                  ISBN 1-56280-073-6     11.95

CACTUS LOVE by Lee Lynch. 192 pp. Stories by the beloved
storyteller.                         ISBN 1-56280-071-X           9.95

SECOND GUESS by Rose Beecham. 216 pp. An Amanda
Valentine Mystery.                        ISBN 1-56280-069-8      9.95

A RAGE OF MAIDENS by Lauren Wright Douglas. 240 pp.
6th Caitlin Reece Mystery.           ISBN 1-56280-068-X          10.95

TRIPLE EXPOSURE by Jackie Calhoun. 224 pp. Romantic
drama involving many characters.     ISBN 1-56280-067-1          10.95

PERSONAL ADS by Robbi Sommers. 176 pp. Sizzling short
stories.                             ISBN 1-56280-059-0          11.95

CROSSWORDS by Penny Sumner. 256 pp. 2nd Victoria Cross
Mystery.                                  ISBN 1-56280-064-7      9.95

SWEET CHERRY WINE by Carol Schmidt. 224 pp. A novel of
suspense.                                 ISBN 1-56280-063-9      9.95

CERTAIN SMILES by Dorothy Tell. 160 pp. Erotic short stories.
                                          ISBN 1-56280-066-3      9.95

EDITED OUT by Lisa Haddock. 224 pp. 1st Carmen Ramirez
Mystery.                                  ISBN 1-56280-077-9      9.95

SMOKEY O by Celia Cohen. 176 pp. Relationships on the
playing field.                            ISBN 1-56280-057-4      9.95

KATHLEEN O'DONALD by Penny Hayes. 256 pp. Rose and
Kathleen find each other and employment in 1909 NYC.
                                          ISBN 1-56280-070-1      9.95

STAYING HOME by Elisabeth Nonas. 256 pp. Molly and Alix
want a baby . . . or do they?             ISBN 1-56280-076-0     10.95

TRUE LOVE by Jennifer Fulton. 240 pp. Six lesbians searching
for love in all the "right" places.             ISBN 1-56280-035-3        11.95

KEEPING SECRETS by Penny Mickelbury. 208 pp. 1st Gianna
Maglione Mystery.                               ISBN 1-56280-052-3         9.95

THE ROMANTIC NAIAD edited by Katherine V. Forrest &
Barbara Grier. 336 pp. Love stories by Naiad Press authors.
                                                ISBN 1-56280-054-X        14.95

UNDER MY SKIN by Jaye Maiman. 336 pp. 3rd Robin Miller
Mystery.                                        ISBN 1-56280-049-3.       11.95

CAR POOL by Karin Kallmaker. 272pp. Lesbians on wheels
and then some!                                  ISBN 1-56280-048-5        11.95

NOT TELLING MOTHER: STORIES FROM A LIFE by Diane
Salvatore. 176 pp. Her 3rd novel.               ISBN 1-56280-044-2         9.95

GOBLIN MARKET by Lauren Wright Douglas. 240pp. 5th Caitlin
Reece Mystery.                                  ISBN 1-56280-047-7        10.95

FRIENDS AND LOVERS by Jackie Calhoun. 224 pp. Mid-
western Lesbian lives and loves.                ISBN 1-56280-041-8        11.95

BEHIND CLOSED DOORS by Robbi Sommers. 192 pp. Hot,
erotic short stories.                           ISBN 1-56280-039-6        11.95

CLAIRE OF THE MOON by Nicole Conn. 192 pp. See the
movie — read the book!                          ISBN 1-56280-038-8        11.95

SILENT HEART by Claire McNab. 192 pp. Exotic Lesbian
romance.                                        ISBN 1-56280-036-1        11.95

THE SPY IN QUESTION by Amanda Kyle Williams. 256 pp.
A Madison McGuire Mystery.                      ISBN 1-56280-037-X         9.95

SAVING GRACE by Jennifer Fulton. 240 pp. Adventure and
romantic entanglement.                          ISBN 1-56280-051-5        11.95

CURIOUS WINE by Katherine V. Forrest. 176 pp. Tenth Anniver-
sary Edition. The most popular contemporary Lesbian love story.
                                                ISBN 1-56280-053-1        11.95
      Audio Book (2 cassettes)                  ISBN 1-56280-105-8        16.95

CHAUTAUQUA by Catherine Ennis. 192 pp. Exciting, romantic
adventure.                                      ISBN 1-56280-032-9         9.95

A PROPER BURIAL by Pat Welch. 192 pp. 3rd Helen Black
Mystery.                                        ISBN 1-56280-033-7         9.95

SILVERLAKE HEAT: A Novel of Suspense by Carol Schmidt.
240 pp. Rhonda is as hot as Laney's dreams.     ISBN 1-56280-031-0         9.95

LOVE, ZENA BETH by Diane Salvatore. 224 pp. The most talked
about lesbian novel of the nineties!            ISBN 1-56280-030-2        10.95

A DOORYARD FULL OF FLOWERS by Isabel Miller. 160 pp.
Stories incl. 2 sequels to *Patience and Sarah*.   ISBN 1-56280-029-9      9.95

MURDER BY TRADITION by Katherine V. Forrest. 288 pp. 4th
Kate Delafield Mystery.                    ISBN 1-56280-002-7    11.95

THE EROTIC NAIAD edited by Katherine V. Forrest & Barbara
Grier. 224 pp. Love stories by Naiad Press authors.
                                          ISBN 1-56280-026-4    14.95

DEAD CERTAIN by Claire McNab. 224 pp. 5th Carol Ashton
Mystery.                                   ISBN 1-56280-027-2     9.95

CRAZY FOR LOVING by Jaye Maiman. 320 pp. 2nd Robin Miller
Mystery.                                   ISBN 1-56280-025-6    11.95

UNCERTAIN COMPANIONS by Robbi Sommers. 204 pp.
Steamy, erotic novel.                      ISBN 1-56280-017-5    11.95

A TIGER'S HEART by Lauren W. Douglas. 240 pp. 4th Caitlin
Reece Mystery.                             ISBN 1-56280-018-3     9.95

PAPERBACK ROMANCE by Karin Kallmaker. 256 pp. A
delicious romance.                         ISBN 1-56280-019-1    10.95

THE LAVENDER HOUSE MURDER by Nikki Baker. 224 pp.
2nd Virginia Kelly Mystery.                ISBN 1-56280-012-4     9.95

PASSION BAY by Jennifer Fulton. 224 pp. Passionate romance,
virgin beaches, tropical skies.            ISBN 1-56280-028-0    10.95

STICKS AND STONES by Jackie Calhoun. 208 pp. Contemporary
lesbian lives and loves.                   ISBN 1-56280-020-5     9.95
Audio Book (2 cassettes)                   ISBN 1-56280-106-6    16.95

UNDER THE SOUTHERN CROSS by Claire McNab. 192 pp.
Romantic nights Down Under.                ISBN 1-56280-011-6    11.95

GRASSY FLATS by Penny Hayes. 256 pp. Lesbian romance in
the '30s.                                  ISBN 1-56280-010-8     9.95

THE END OF APRIL by Penny Sumner. 240 pp. 1st Victoria
Cross Mystery.                             ISBN 1-56280-007-8     8.95

KISS AND TELL by Robbi Sommers. 192 pp. Scorching stories
by the author of *Pleasures*.              ISBN 1-56280-005-1    11.95

STILL WATERS by Pat Welch. 208 pp. 2nd Helen Black Mystery.
                                          ISBN 0-941483-97-5     9.95

TO LOVE AGAIN by Evelyn Kennedy. 208 pp. Wildly romantic
love story.                                ISBN 0-941483-85-1    11.95

IN THE GAME by Nikki Baker. 192 pp. 1st Virginia Kelly
Mystery.                                   ISBN 1-56280-004-3     9.95

STRANDED by Camarin Grae. 320 pp. Entertaining, riveting
adventure.                                 ISBN 0-941483-99-1     9.95

THE DAUGHTERS OF ARTEMIS by Lauren Wright Douglas.
240 pp. 3rd Caitlin Reece Mystery.         ISBN 0-941483-95-9     9.95

CLEARWATER by Catherine Ennis. 176 pp. Romantic secrets
of a small Louisiana town.                 ISBN 0-941483-65-7     8.95

THE HALLELUJAH MURDERS by Dorothy Tell. 176 pp. 2nd
Poppy Dillworth Mystery. ISBN 0-941483-88-6   8.95

BENEDICTION by Diane Salvatore. 272 pp. Striking, contemporary romantic novel. ISBN 0-941483-90-8   11.95

COP OUT by Claire McNab. 208 pp. 4th Carol Ashton Mystery.
ISBN 0-941483-84-3   10.95

THE BEVERLY MALIBU by Katherine V. Forrest. 288 pp. 3rd
Kate Delafield Mystery. ISBN 0-941483-48-7   11.95

THE PROVIDENCE FILE by Amanda Kyle Williams. 256 pp.
A Madison McGuire Mystery. ISBN 0-941483-92-4   8.95

I LEFT MY HEART by Jaye Maiman. 320 pp. 1st Robin Miller
Mystery. ISBN 0-941483-72-X   11.95

THE PRICE OF SALT by Patricia Highsmith (writing as Claire
Morgan). 288 pp. Classic lesbian novel, first issued in 1952 . . .
acknowledged by its author under her own, very famous, name.
ISBN 1-56280-003-5   11.95

SIDE BY SIDE by Isabel Miller. 256 pp. From beloved author of
*Patience and Sarah.* ISBN 0-941483-77-0   10.95

STAYING POWER: LONG TERM LESBIAN COUPLES by
Susan E. Johnson. 352 pp. Joys of coupledom. ISBN 0-941-483-75-4   14.95

SLICK by Camarin Grae. 304 pp. Exotic, erotic adventure.
ISBN 0-941483-74-6   9.95

NINTH LIFE by Lauren Wright Douglas. 256 pp. 2nd Caitlin
Reece Mystery. ISBN 0-941483-50-9   9.95

PLAYERS by Robbi Sommers. 192 pp. Sizzling, erotic novel.
ISBN 0-941483-73-8   9.95

MURDER AT RED ROOK RANCH by Dorothy Tell. 224 pp.
1st Poppy Dillworth Mystery. ISBN 0-941483-80-0   8.95

A ROOM FULL OF WOMEN by Elisabeth Nonas. 256 pp.
Contemporary Lesbian lives. ISBN 0-941483-69-X   9.95

THEME FOR DIVERSE INSTRUMENTS by Jane Rule. 208 pp.
Powerful romantic lesbian stories. ISBN 0-941483-63-0   8.95

CLUB 12 by Amanda Kyle Williams. 288 pp. Espionage thriller
featuring a lesbian agent! ISBN 0-941483-64-9   9.95

DEATH DOWN UNDER by Claire McNab. 240 pp. 3rd Carol
Ashton Mystery. ISBN 0-941483-39-8   10.95

MONTANA FEATHERS by Penny Hayes. 256 pp. Vivian and
Elizabeth find love in frontier Montana. ISBN 0-941483-61-4   9.95

THERE'S SOMETHING I'VE BEEN MEANING TO TELL YOU
Ed. by Loralee MacPike. 288 pp. Gay men and lesbians coming out
to their children. ISBN 0-941483-44-4   9.95

LIFTING BELLY by Gertrude Stein. Ed. by Rebecca Mark. 104 pp.
Erotic poetry.                          ISBN 0-941483-51-7      10.95

AFTER THE FIRE by Jane Rule. 256 pp. Warm, human novel by
this incomparable author.               ISBN 0-941483-45-2       8.95

PLEASURES by Robbi Sommers. 204 pp. Unprecedented
eroticism.                              ISBN 0-941483-49-5      11.95

EDGEWISE by Camarin Grae. 372 pp. Spellbinding
adventure.                              ISBN 0-941483-19-3       9.95

FATAL REUNION by Claire McNab. 224 pp. 2nd Carol Ashton
Mystery.                                ISBN 0-941483-40-1      11.95

IN EVERY PORT by Karin Kallmaker. 228 pp. Jessica's sexy,
adventuresome travels.                  ISBN 0-941483-37-7      11.95

OF LOVE AND GLORY by Evelyn Kennedy. 192 pp. Exciting
WWII romance.                           ISBN 0-941483-32-0      10.95

CLICKING STONES by Nancy Tyler Glenn. 288 pp. Love
transcending time.                      ISBN 0-941483-31-2       9.95

SOUTH OF THE LINE by Catherine Ennis. 216 pp. Civil War
adventure.                              ISBN 0-941483-29-0       8.95

WOMAN PLUS WOMAN by Dolores Klaich. 300 pp. Supurb
Lesbian overview.                       ISBN 0-941483-28-2       9.95

THE FINER GRAIN by Denise Ohio. 216 pp. Brilliant young
college lesbian novel.                  ISBN 0-941483-11-8       8.95

LESSONS IN MURDER by Claire McNab. 216 pp. 1st Carol Ashton
Mystery.                                ISBN 0-941483-14-2      11.95

YELLOWTHROAT by Penny Hayes. 240 pp. Margarita, bandit,
kidnaps Julia.                          ISBN 0-941483-10-X       8.95

SAPPHISTRY: THE BOOK OF LESBIAN SEXUALITY by
Pat Califia. 3d edition, revised. 208 pp.   ISBN 0-941483-24-X   12.95

CHERISHED LOVE by Evelyn Kennedy. 192 pp. Erotic Lesbian
love story.                             ISBN 0-941483-08-8      11.95

THE SECRET IN THE BIRD by Camarin Grae. 312 pp. Striking,
psychological suspense novel.           ISBN 0-941483-05-3       8.95

TO THE LIGHTNING by Catherine Ennis. 208 pp. Romantic
Lesbian `Robinson Crusoe adventure.     ISBN 0-941483-06-1       8.95

DREAMS AND SWORDS by Katherine V. Forrest. 192 pp.
Romantic, erotic, imaginative stories.  ISBN 0-941483-03-7      11.95

MEMORY BOARD by Jane Rule. 336 pp. Memorable novel
about an aging Lesbian couple.          ISBN 0-941483-02-9      12.95

THE ALWAYS ANONYMOUS BEAST by Lauren Wright Douglas.
224 pp. 1st Caitlin Reece Mystery.      ISBN 0-941483-04-5       8.95

MURDER AT THE NIGHTWOOD BAR by Katherine V. Forrest.
240  pp. 2nd Kate Delafield Mystery.    ISBN 0-930044-92-4      11.95

WINGED DANCER by Camarin Grae. 228 pp. Erotic Lesbian
adventure story.                                ISBN 0-930044-88-6        8.95

PAZ by Camarin Grae. 336 pp. Romantic Lesbian adventurer
with the power to change the world.            ISBN 0-930044-89-4        8.95

SOUL SNATCHER by Camarin Grae. 224 pp. A puzzle, an
adventure, a mystery — Lesbian romance.        ISBN 0-930044-90-8        8.95

THE LOVE OF GOOD WOMEN by Isabel Miller. 224 pp.
Long-awaited new novel by the author of the beloved *Patience
and Sarah*.                                    ISBN 0-930044-81-9        8.95

THE LONG TRAIL by Penny Hayes. 248 pp. Vivid adventures
of two women in love in the old west.          ISBN 0-930044-76-2        8.95

AN EMERGENCE OF GREEN by Katherine V. Forrest. 288
pp. Powerful novel of sexual discovery.        ISBN 0-930044-69-X       11.95

DESERT OF THE HEART by Jane Rule. 224 pp. A classic;
basis for the movie *Desert Hearts*.           ISBN 0-930044-73-8       10.95

SEX VARIANT WOMEN IN LITERATURE by Jeannette
Howard Foster. 448 pp. Literary history.       ISBN 0-930044-65-7        8.95

A HOT-EYED MODERATE by Jane Rule. 252 pp. Hard-hitting
essays on gay life; writing; art.              ISBN 0-930044-57-6        7.95

AMATEUR CITY by Katherine V. Forrest. 224 pp. 1st Kate
Delafield Mystery.                             ISBN 0-930044-55-X       10.95

THE SOPHIE HOROWITZ STORY by Sarah Schulman. 176 pp.
Engaging novel of madcap intrigue.             ISBN 0-930044-54-1        7.95

THE YOUNG IN ONE ANOTHER'S ARMS by Jane Rule.
224 pp. Classic Jane Rule.                     ISBN 0-930044-53-3        9.95

AGAINST THE SEASON by Jane Rule. 224 pp. Luminous,
complex novel of interrelationships.           ISBN 0-930044-48-7        8.95

LOVERS IN THE PRESENT AFTERNOON by Kathleen Fleming.
288 pp. A novel about recovery and growth.     ISBN 0-930044-46-0        8.95

THIS IS NOT FOR YOU by Jane Rule. 284 pp. A letter to a
beloved is also an intricate novel.            ISBN 0-930044-25-8        8.95

OUTLANDER by Jane Rule. 207 pp. Short stories and essays by
one of our finest writers.                     ISBN 0-930044-17-7        8.95

These are just a few of the many Naiad Press titles — we are the oldest and
largest lesbian/feminist publishing company in the world. We also offer an
enormous selection of lesbian video products. Please request a complete
catalog. We offer personal service; we encourage and welcome direct mail
orders from individuals who have limited access to bookstores carrying our
publications.